THE CAR

THE CAR

Gary Paulsen

〰〰〰〰〰〰

Harcourt Brace & Company

SAN DIEGO   NEW YORK   LONDON

Requests for permission to make copies of any part of the work should be mailed to: Permissions Department, Harcourt Brace & Company, 6277 Sea Harbor Drive, Orlando, Florida 32887–6777.

Library of Congress Cataloging-in-Publication Data
Paulsen, Gary.
The car/Gary Paulsen.—1st ed.
p. cm.
Summary: A teenager left on his own travels west in a kit car he built himself, and along the way picks up two Vietnam veterans, who take him on an eye-opening journey.
ISBN 0-15-292878-2
[1. Automobiles—Fiction. 2. Travel—Fiction. 3. Vietnamese Conflict, 1961–1975—Veterans—Fiction.] I. Title.
PZ7.P2843Car 1994
[Fic]—dc20   93-41834

Printed in the United States of America

Designed by Lydia D'moch

D F G E

To Stuart, whose name is on The Wall

THE CAR

THE CAR

〰〰〰〰〰

MEMORIES

It was to be a normal strike mission. Another hamlet, another set of leaders to take out—sanction, neutralize, terminate with extreme prejudice. All names for the same thing—to kill. There were two of them in the strike team, and they had done this before and expected no real difficulties.

Come in the darkness by canoe let off from the patrol boat on the main river. Paddle up the small stream to the hamlet, find the two targets, end them, and canoe back to the patrol boat.

In and out.

"Clean and gone," one of the strike team members said. "They won't know we've been there until they find the bodies. . . ."

1

He was alone.

His name was Terry Anders. He was fourteen years old, living in Cleveland, Ohio, and his parents had left him.

Of course it didn't happen quite that suddenly.

It was true he could not exactly remember a happy time with his parents. He thought there might have been a few moments when he was a baby, but they weren't memories so much as feelings, or wishes about feelings he would have liked to have had.

But most of it had been a hassle. All he knew was their fighting. His earliest memory was of them fighting. They never hurt him, never yelled at him much; they just ignored him. They were two people who just shouldn't have been together.

He had been ignored for fourteen years. Completely. They didn't care how he did, what he wore, what he ate, if he was sick or well or doing all right in school or flunking. They weren't bad to him, nor good to him, nor anything to him. At first it bothered him, but he had become accustomed to it and, finally, had come to prefer it.

He felt that as far as his parents were concerned he simply didn't exist and he viewed them the same. There were no other children, no contact with relatives except an uncle or something—Terry was never sure of the relationship to his parents—out in Oregon. Terry had met him once—back when he was six or seven—and the uncle, named Loren, seemed like a nice guy. He had given Terry five dollars and told him to buy candy.

Other than that, nothing. Nobody. His parents both worked at jobs—his father as a mechanic at a car dealership, his mother as a beautician—and were gone during weekdays. On weekends his father would leave at sunup to go four-wheeling with his friends, and his mother would hit the malls and shop—or something. Terry was never quite sure of that, either, since she never seemed to bring anything home.

Terry was left to himself. He worked at school some but mostly had poor grades, kind of slithered by. He'd had a best friend named Thor, but Thor's family had moved just a month before to—of all places—Africa, where Thor's father was going to be a missionary, and so Terry was alone.

He didn't honestly know his parents were gone for nearly two days. He woke up one Monday morning to a quiet house—his parents had spent the whole previous

night yelling at each other and the quiet was pleasant—
and went about his day as usual, figuring his parents had
gone to work.

Breakfast that first morning was normal. Sugar-
coated cereal with milk and more sugar sprinkled on it.
There was no bread so he couldn't do toast and peanut
butter, which he loved, but the cereal filled him so it
didn't matter.

Through the day he worked at mowing lawns in a
nearby housing development. He loved working with
motors and mechanical devices—he sometimes thought
it was the only thing he got from his father—and had
rebuilt an old rotary lawn mower that he used for cutting
grass. The business had started small but had grown, and
he had saved almost thirteen hundred dollars over the
last two years, which he kept in a jar in his room.

Terry worked all day, and when it was evening he
pushed the mower home to find his parents still not
there.

Again, this did not surprise him. They were often
late, and sometimes his father did not come home at all.

They lived in a rented old two-story house on the
edge of an open field at the end of a road near a housing
development, and all of it seemed about to break down
and die. The house was in need of paint and repair, the
street coming from the development was full of potholes
and cracks, and the land around was overgrown with
weeds and brush.

When he got home Terry put the mower in the garage, went into the house, and turned the TV set on to
some rerun of a reran rerun about kids in the sixties,
who all wore bell-bottom pants and long-collared shirts.

He didn't much like television—it bored him, except for the music videos and some movies—but he kept it on all the time he was in the house because he needed the sound. He'd read something in school about certain people needing background sound like running water or surf or wind in trees—they called it "white" sound—and he thought of television that way. Pretty much worthless except as "white" sound.

He found TV dinners and cooked two of them (one was never enough)—turkey loaf and beef stew—and ate them watching the show about the kids in the sixties. He watched more TV and worked on a model of a '57 Chevy he'd been putting together for two weeks. He liked working on models—when he couldn't work on engines—because it completely occupied his mind, making them look exact, clean, dead perfect. Then somehow it was night and his parents still weren't home, and he went to bed.

The second morning he awakened to the same routine, but now there was wonder—they should have been home and fighting by this time—and he thought about calling somebody like the police. But something stopped him. A little tickle, a happiness at the quiet and peace was there in his mind, and he didn't make the call but went out again to mow lawns.

That evening they were still not home, and he sat quietly working on the model after two more TV dinners, and for the first time he thought of the movie about the kid who was left home by himself. Except that the same tickle was there, the feeling that it was actually nice not having them around.

The first call came at almost exactly eight o'clock.

His mother called first.

"Terry, I'm not coming home. I can't take it any longer. I've taken all my things. Tell your father I won't be there for him to fight any longer. You'll both have to do without me." And she hung up.

He had said almost nothing. Had once more felt a sense of wonder—this time at why he didn't seem to care all that much that his mother had gone. A part of him felt bad, but it was mostly because he *didn't* feel bad that he felt bad—like he ought to feel rotten, only he didn't. She was gone—that thought was there—and there wouldn't be any more fights.

His father called just after nine.

"Tell your mother I'm not coming back—I've got all my stuff, or everything I want. I'm sick of the whole thing." And he hung up.

Terry put the phone back in the cradle and looked out the window at the road in the darkness and thought: *So, they aren't going to be here. Neither one. At least for a little while. Mother thinks I'm staying here with Father and Father thinks I'm staying here with Mother.*

I'm alone.

Just me.

And the house.

Oh yes, he thought, and a smile came, widened into a grin. *There's one other thing.*

The car.

2

THE CAR WASN'T REALLY.

A car that is—it was a pile of what seemed to be
junk and pieces in the garage. At some point along the
way, Terry's father had done some work for a trucker,
and the man hadn't had enough money to pay for the
work and had given Terry's father the car in partial payment. Terry's father had objected, had threatened to go
to court, had even had a fight with the man—a scuffle
in the driveway—but it didn't help. The trucker had left
the car as payment and gone on his way.

It was a kit car, supposedly a design done by a man
named Blakely, called a Blakely Bearcat—a soft red color
with sweeping curved-back fenders and the classic old-
fashioned open-cockpit look.

Or it should have been. The truth was Terry's dad

hated being a mechanic. When his day at work was done, the last thing he wanted to do was pick up a wrench and work on a home project. He had tried to sell the kit as it was—piles of red fiberglass pieces and rusting steel frames and paper-wrapped chrome trim—but nobody wanted it. Several came to look and just shrugged and walked away when they saw the mess. The result was that the pile of parts stayed a pile that didn't resemble any part of a car so much as a start for a junkyard, and over the months, almost a year and a half, nothing had been done to make the kit a car.

Once Terry had asked his father if he could work on the Bearcat.

"No," his father had answered. "I'm going to let it sit there and rot, and every time I look at the thing it will remind me to always get the money up front."

And so it had been. The Bearcat—Terry always thought of it simply as the Cat—had remained a pile for all this time. Well, twice he had peeked into it when both parents were gone for the day—dug around in the boxes and crates and paper-wrapped pieces to see what was involved in making a car. He was, to be honest, dying to get into it. But anything he did would certainly be seen by his father, who had expressly forbidden Terry to work on the car.

But his father was gone now. He'd said he wasn't coming back. And the same for his mother.

And the kit car was still in the garage.

He looked once at the clock on the kitchen wall. It was in the shape of a cat with eyes that went back and forth and the hands were in a circle on the cat's belly. It was, Terry thought, the ugliest thing he had probably ever seen. He had bought it for a Christmas present when he was nine years old, trying to get his mother's attention. It hadn't worked except that she'd put the clock on the wall over the kitchen window where Terry could see it every day.

Nine-thirty.

He could, of course, sit and watch television—the thought hit him even as he was moving toward the door that led to the garage. He could sit and watch the tube and munch on some junk, or he could go to bed because it was getting late, or . . .

He opened the door to the garage, pulled the cord that turned on the overhead light, and looked at the pile near the wall.

Yeah, he thought. *I could go to bed or watch the tube, or I could go over there and just take a look at what's involved.*

He went to the workbench at the end of the garage where he worked on his mower. He had a complete set of tools—sockets and wrenches, feeler gauges, everything to work on motors. He'd bought the set at a rummage sale for thirty dollars two years before without knowing how complete the set was; it had belonged to an old man who had passed away, who had done all his own work on his car, and the tools were so complete they included a torque wrench and special deep-well sockets. There was even a small dental mirror for looking up in hard-to-see places, and everything, from the mirror to the largest wrench, every tool had been kept in top condition.

Terry kept them the same way. He'd bought a large bag of clean red mechanics' rags at the discount store and each time he used a tool he wiped it carefully before putting it back.

His toolbox was the kind that sat upright with four drawers that pulled out, and he moved to the box now and opened the top, pulled the drawers out, and made sure—as he always did—that the tools were all there.

Then he turned to the car.

The boxes and parts were in a haphazard pile on top of the frame. The man who had initially owned the kit car had done some basic work on it. The frame was bolted and welded together correctly and the wheels and tires had been put on. The motor and transmission were also bolted into position on the frame, set in rubber motor mounts, and the drive shaft was in place back to the rear differential, but none of the body was on nor any of the controls for the wheels or motor. The car sat on the floor on tires—the frame, the motor—and stacked on top was the rest of the car in torn paper wrapping and cardboard boxes.

"Let's see what we've got . . . ," Terry said under his breath and started taking the boxes off, setting them around the garage on the floor, looking in each one as he did so.

Much of the stuff he couldn't identify. There were large boxes with the fenders, the rear trunk lid, the hood (tags called the hood a bonnet and the trunk lid a boot), doors, interior panels, molded black dashboard, windshield. All of that he knew, could understand, but there were numbered bags and boxes with just bolts and parts, and many of them made no sense to him, and he despaired of ever understanding it all when in the bottom of one of the boxes he found the instructions.

They were in the form of a book or magazine and seemed incredibly complete, explaining things in detail with step-by-step instructions and with photos to show each step being accomplished.

"A monkey could do this," he said, sitting on the frame, going page by page. "You don't have to know anything about cars at all. It's beautiful. . . ."

Not only were the instructions complete but they explained what was in each numbered box or bag—what each set of bolts was for—and he set about organizing all of them to get ready for starting work on the car.

Time seemed to stop while he worked. He used a notebook to catalog and place items, writing them down as he put them in order on the garage floor, and after a period he felt hungry and went into the kitchen for some lunch meat. Once he started to eat he was amazed at his hunger and he looked up to the cat clock, stunned to see that it was three in the morning.

I should feel tired, he thought, but the sandwich seemed to give him energy, and he moved back to the garage to start work on the car.

MEMORIES

Initially the strike went as planned, was so smooth it seemed choreographed.

The river patrol boat dropped them with their canoe, where the stream from the hamlet entered the main river. They were dressed in black, with black hats and black camouflage makeup. They did not smile and squinted so the whites of their eyes didn't show, and against the black wall of the Vietnamese jungle they simply did not exist.

One of them bumped a paddle on the side of the flat black canoe and the other hissed a curse at the thumping sound, but they were still far from the hamlet—4.7 kilometers, according to the map they had studied when planning the strike—and there was nobody to hear the sound.

They moved away from the patrol boat, working their paddles silently without taking them from the water, and within a hundred feet they were part of the night. . . .

3

He went to the instructions again, starting with page one, picture one, working against what had already been done, double-checking what the original owner had completed.

He didn't know the man's name at first, but a few minutes after he started, a piece of paper fell out of the instruction book with the name Tom Haskell written on it, and he thought of the owner as Tom after that.

Whatever the name was, Terry admired his work. The things that were done were done right. Bolts on the motor mount were torqued to the correct foot-pounds of torque. Everything was aligned properly, squared, and checked, but when Terry was working on the radiator, checking to see if all the hoses were there, the lack of sleep caught up with him.

He closed his eyes—to blink, nothing more—and they just didn't open again. He slept sitting on the frame, his forehead against the radiator, which was braced across his knees, for nearly two hours.

When he awakened, his legs were asleep because the radiator had cut off the circulation, and he stood carefully, went back into the house—walking like Frankenstein—and drank the last of the milk.

It was eight in the morning. He'd worked all night, except for the two hours' sleep. His brain was still numb and he went to the couch, flicked the remote to turn the television on, and fell asleep in the middle of a game show.

The ringing phone awakened him and he was sitting up, grabbing for the receiver on the end table, before he was fully awake.

"Hello?"

"Mr. Anders?"

"Uhh . . . yes."

"Your phone bill is two and a half months past due, Mr. Anders. Could we expect some payment on it this week?"

"Well, see, the truth is . . ." Terry didn't know what to say.

"The thing is, Mr. Anders, if you don't pay on it, I'm afraid we'll have to cut service."

Terry was fully awake now and realized what had happened. His mother and father had let bills go before they left. He lowered his voice, tried to sound older. "I understand."

"All we can give you is another two weeks."

"Fine."

"Then you'll send some money?"

"I'll do what I can."

"Thank you, Mr. Anders."

Terry hung up and stood. Between sitting and standing the whole conversation on the phone left his mind.

The car.

He had to work on the car.

He went to the kitchen and ate some lunch meat. There was some mustard in a jar and he smeared it on the meat before eating it, and while still chewing he made his way to the garage where the car waited.

He was at the point where the body had to be right to give him places to bolt new things—like putting the radiator in place. It needed side mounts to hold it, and without the engine compartment there would be no side mounts.

He started with the compartment itself, bolting the red side panels onto the frame, squirting thread-lock on each nut to make sure they wouldn't vibrate loose later, even though he was also using lock washers.

With the compartment in place the pieces started to look like a car, and he stepped back to study it.

He smiled. Not much of a car, but there was a shape coming, a look to it. The side compartments on the engine, where the sweeping fenders would bolt on, gave the kit the beginning look of a car, started to show some of the curves.

He finished bolting the radiator in place, adjusting it to clear the blades of the fan mounted on the front of the engine. The hoses from the radiator to the engine and back took some work, but Tom had ordered them right, and by twisting and turning and warping them, Terry finally got them into position and clamped on tightly.

Steering was next. The tie rods and steering gear were already in place on the frame, but there was no wheel or shaft coming through the fire wall to steer the car with. He found the shaft and turn indicator bracket but there was no wheel, and the whole assembly was obviously from another car—as were the engine and wheels.

For a moment it threw him until he found the title of ownership in a plastic bag taped in place in the back of the instruction manual.

All the parts not from the kit—the four-cylinder engine, the wheels and tires, the steering column, and the brakes—were from a 1974 Ford Pinto. The title and papers from the original car were in the plastic bag along with a note from a machinist:

"Tom," Terry read aloud, "I've gone completely over the engine and rebuilt it to tighter tolerances than they have in the factory. It will be better than new. Just break it in slow, real slow, and let the rings seat on their own without pushing it."

And in a last box, leaning against the inside of the frame and hidden from view, Terry found the steering wheel.

"It's beautiful. . . ." He spoke aloud when he opened the box. The wheel was black leather, polished and hand-rubbed, with brushed stainless steel spokes. In the middle was a horn ring with the Bearcat emblem in the center. There were also complete instructions on how to mount the steering wheel, and he put it in just because it looked good, even though the dash wasn't quite complete yet and all the instruments weren't hooked up.

When the wheel was in and lined up right and tightened down, he stepped back and looked at the overall car again. Having the wheel in place gave it an even more complete look, and he smiled, almost laughed.

He was going to have a car.

It was right there. All the rest of what he needed was right there in front of him. The parts just needed to be bolted together.

But right now he was hungry—worse, *starved*—and there was nothing in the house. He took ten dollars from his stash and rode his bicycle to the supermarket nine blocks away, and all the way, with every push and pull of his foot on the pedal of the bike, he thought, *Next time I go to the store I'll take the Cat.*

4

THE CAR SEEMED DONE.

Terry had lost track of time. He sat on the step leading from the house to the garage, drinking milk directly out of the carton and eating lunch meat rolled in a tube and dipped in peanut butter and then swirled in a mustard jar.

The grimy window at the side of the garage showed it to be dark outside. Other than that he had no idea of how long he'd been working. He'd stopped to sleep several times, catching naps on the couch or chairs, once sleeping for an hour or so sitting in the black leather seat of the Cat, looking over the hood before he'd attached the windshield.

It was done.

But it was like a large model. Or a toy, like Pinoc-

chio. Pretty, but without life. It sat gleaming in the overhead light, beautiful curved lines and streamlined shape,
looking more like an updated version of the old 1950
MGs. An almost square radiator grill, a flat windshield
angled slightly back so it wouldn't catch the wind, doors
that dropped so low it was possible to sit in the car and
easily touch the ground, shiny silver-spoked wheels,
chrome stand-alone headlights, and a squarish back and
trunk lid with a chromed luggage rack. There was no
top, no cover of any kind from the weather.

"Do you run?" Terry asked the car, not feeling
strange in the least that he was talking to the Cat. He
had spoken to it all the time when he was building it,
sometimes smiling, sometimes swearing when something
didn't fit quite right. Installing the interior carpeting and
dash padding had been a headache as had the gas tank,
which he was still worried about. "Will you start and
run?"

He got in the car and sat in the driver's seat, looking
at the instrument panel. Hooking everything up had
been easier than he'd thought. There was a wire harness
with all the correct jacks and plugs from various parts of
the engine to the VDO instruments on the dash. They
were easy to read, black with white letters and needles,
and the tachometer had an adjustable fluorescent orange
indicator where redline should be. Lights, indicators,
everything was hooked up.

But the battery was dead, or nearly so, and while it
made the lights work well enough, Terry wasn't sure
there'd be enough juice to get the motor turning to fire
the ignition.

He decided to use a trick he did with small motors

when they'd been sitting a long time. He raised the hood—it went up forward—and propped it with the two metal arms that popped into little side brackets in the hood. The motor looked clean enough to eat from, and he unscrewed the top of the air cleaner and removed the cover to open the throat of the carburetor.

By the workbench he had a five-gallon gas container he'd carried from the gas station on the corner. Most of the gas he'd already poured into the small opening of the filler cap for the Cat. But he'd saved some, and he poured half a cup in an empty soda bottle.

He held the choke plate open in the carburetor with his finger and trickled a couple of tablespoons of the gas from the soda bottle directly into the carburetor.

He quickly jumped into the driver's seat, turned the key on, and pushed it over to the start position.

The motor growled lowly, hesitated, seemed to almost stop, and then fired with an explosion, shooting a spurt of flame out the top of the carburetor that lit up the whole interior of the garage and made Terry jump four inches out of the seat.

Then it died.

But before it died it turned over six or seven times. It was enough to turn on the water pump and get the antifreeze moving through the system, and it also worked the fuel pump and brought gas up from the tank to fill the line to the carburetor.

Terry took the soda bottle and dripped a bit of gas into the top of the carburetor throat, then sat in the seat again and reached for the key.

He crossed his fingers. "Come on—there's almost nothing left in the battery. One time."

He turned the key to start.

Another low growl, the battery dying, the engine turning, grinding, and Terry started to shake his head, knowing it wouldn't go.

It fired again, shot flames out the top of the carburetor as it had at first, but this time it sucked gas from the line back down in, pulled air in, and the motor started with a bellowing roar out the glass-packed, straight-line muffler.

"Yes!" Terry said, his foot on the accelerator. He revved the engine gently a couple of times, then remembered he had the garage door closed and he was about to gas himself. He left the car running and opened the garage door and discovered it was starting to turn gray in the east. Early morning. It must be about four, he thought, or maybe three-thirty.

He went back to the car—he thought of it always as the Cat now—and checked the gauges. Oil was running at 60 psi, battery charging—he had had no idea if the alternator would work or not and was glad it seemed to be all right—and the tachometer showed the car to be idling at about 700 rpm. Just a hair slow, according to the instruction book, but he would adjust it later.

Everything seemed to be working right, and he shook his head. It couldn't be that easy to build a car. Something had to be wrong.

He pushed the clutch down, put the Cat in reverse, and remembered he'd never driven a straight-stick car before. In fact he'd only driven a car three times—when his friend Thor's father had let them both drive out in the country on a dirt road.

He let the clutch out and the car jerked backward once and stalled and died.

"Come on, Cat. . . ."

He put it in neutral and started it again, pleased when it kicked right off. Once more the clutch in, the stick to reverse—he eased the clutch out and gave it a little gas and it slid backward half a car length before dying again, the rear end of the car hanging out of the garage.

"Damn."

One more try, he thought. *How hard can it be? People do it all the time.*

Neutral, restart, clutch in, reverse, and more gas this time, lots of gas, run the tach up to almost 2000 rpm— he thought of it as two grand—and he popped the clutch.

Too fast.

The car hesitated, seemed almost to die once more, then caught the gas and overcame the inertia of sitting still and went for it.

He was doing almost thirty miles an hour, in reverse, when he hit the street.

He had been watching to the rear over the trunk lid, but the sudden lurch whipped his head around and for a critical second he was looking forward while moving backward at a high rate of speed.

When he swung his head back around to the rear he was in the street and perfectly lined up on a Toyota pickup parked along the curb, the Cat's rear end aimed at the dead center of the Toyota's door.

Terry pulled the wheel over to the left, hitting the

brakes at the same time. The Cat responded instantly—the steering was less than one to one; three-quarters of a turn on the wheel turned the front wheels all the way over. The front end slewed around like it was on ice. With a screeching sound loud enough to wake people three blocks away, the Cat slid sideways and stopped just four inches from the pickup, nose to tail, hung there for half a second while Terry slammed the clutch in, jerked the stick into first, tromped the accelerator down—what magazine article had taught him *that?*—and popped the clutch.

The Cat held half a beat, then the gas caught and the rear wheels squealed, just a squeak, and Terry was moving forward like he'd been driving all his life.

It was a shade soft in the back. The jerk forward changed the center of gravity and threw some of the weight back, and the Cat began to fishtail. Terry started to correct but the direct steering was fast, too fast, and it worsened the situation until within fifty feet the Cat threatened to swerve violently.

He let up on the gas—unconsciously selecting the right corrective technique—and the Cat lined out, headed up the middle of the street.

He wrapped it up to twenty or so—the pipes were really loud in the still morning between the rows of houses—worked the clutch and caught second (he was already getting smoother on it), and let the Cat line out while he gave it a little gas.

It did more than turn fast. According to the manuals, the car weighed only 1800 pounds. The 2300 cc motor in it was made for a vehicle that came in at 2600 pounds or better, and the light weight of the Cat coupled with the high compression of the newly rebuilt engine and the direct linkage of the straight stick made it almost leap forward.

He hit forty almost at once, saw the tach nudging 3500 rpm—the manual said to keep it below 3000 rpm for five hundred miles—and shifted into third. But he was still in a residential district and he didn't want to go too fast, so he backed down and drove around two blocks in third gear, hardly above an idle.

The Cat drove like a dream. It was tight and low and rode hard—even little cracks in the road seemed to come up through the car into his seat—but it cornered absolutely flat and was so responsive it seemed to be tied to his mind. He could think about turning and it started to go, or so it seemed, and he decided almost at once he didn't care if he ever did anything but drive this car.

Halfway around the second block he heard a hissing sound over the engine noise and the crackling pipes and suddenly smoke came boiling back from beneath the hood, obscuring the windshield. At the same time the engine started to miss and the Cat began to jerk and nearly stopped.

"What the . . . ?"

He shifted down, almost lost it as the Cat stopped, dead. Then it surged again as the engine caught some more life, and he limped back to the garage in low gear, at five miles an hour or less, smoke pouring out of the hood, Terry leaning out the side to see around the windshield, the engine sputtering and threatening to die altogether at any moment. He was intensely glad that nobody seemed to be up yet.

He opened the hood and the garage filled with a

cloud, and in the mist he smelled it and knew it wasn't smoke but antifreeze.

There was a leak somewhere and it had spewed antifreeze all over the engine. The heat immediately turned it to steam and the cooling relief opening around the back of the hood that sucked air over the engine pulled the steam back and out over the windshield along with the heat, and it seemed much worse than it was.

Terry pulled the hood up and all the way over, letting it hang out to the front on the two pivot arms, his forehead frowning in worry.

He had taken the engine for granted. After reading the letter from the machinist he just assumed everything would be all right.

It was a mistake he wouldn't make again.

He used the last of the paper towels—the house was beginning to seem like nobody lived there; everything was running out—to damp-dry the engine, then ate the last of the lunch meat while it cooled.

When the engine and radiator and hoses had cooled to the touch he started searching. He grabbed and tried to wiggle each connection on the line and within moments had found it. The thermostat housing was loose—the bolts only finger-tight—and the gasket had broken away.

It wasn't hard to fix. He used rubber gasket material to cut a new one, using the old one as a pattern, then smeared both sides with nonhardening gasket sealer before putting it back and bolting it down tightly.

But it made all the other connections and fittings suspect and he started over. He found loose bolts on the valve-cover gasket and a small oil leak had developed.

He tightened them, then crawled underneath and checked the pan bolts, found three of them loose as well and tightened them.

He went over the motor four times, checked every bolt and nut, tightened the loose ones, then covered the car end to end twice more and found three others.

At last he was done, and by this time it was late afternoon. He had finished putting on the trunk (the "boot") lid and happened to be standing near the rear of the car when he saw a potential problem.

There was no license plate.

It threw him. He didn't have a driver's license because he was too young, and because of that he couldn't get a plate and couldn't be legal.

He smiled ruefully and shrugged. *Actually*, he thought, *I can't be legal anyway without a license. But with a plate there's a chance I won't be stopped when I drive. . . .*

West.

The word slipped in, just happened, but when it came he realized he'd been thinking of it all the time he'd been working on the car.

He wanted to see the West. His parents wouldn't be checking on him, and if they did they would just assume the other one had him—at least for a while. Until he was gone. Neither of them wanted him much, and if the truth were known he was much happier being alone than with them. And if he went to the authorities it would just be a foster home or something.

He didn't want that.

And it wasn't like he was hitting the streets. He had some money, he could work.

And he had the car.

The Cat.

Maybe they would go out and see the uncle he barely remembered. He touched the car on the front fender and smiled as he realized he thought of himself and the car in terms of *we*.

Yeah. We'll go out and see the uncle.

We'll head west.

But there was this little problem with the plate to work out first.

Memories

Up the small stream, making absolutely no sound as the stream grew narrower and narrower—it took them an hour to reach their destination.

Without speaking they both stopped paddling at the same time, let the canoe come to the shore next to the hamlet.

In truth not even a hamlet. During the intelligence briefing it was called a hamlet but that was a misnomer. Really it was a collection of grass-and-leaf shacks along a river with no electricity, no water, no sewers, and exactly thirty-one people who spent the force of their entire lives trying to make a living out of nearby rice paddies.

It was not possible. The rains came wrong or didn't come at all, the war came wrong all the time, disease hit the rice and the people, babies kept coming, and there was never enough rice to keep them anything other than thin.

The team had come to kill two of the people in the collection of shacks.

That was its job, the team. To kill people. Village leaders who were working for the Communists, selected men and women who were suspected of working for the Communist cadre, people that somebody didn't like or approve of—the team killed them.

They were called the Phoenix Teams and that was their job, to kill people.

This night there were two men in the team just as there were two men to kill, but they were not to split up. They would both be at the killing of each man.

The killing was a simple thing, a stupid thing to have so much importance given to it. The two-man team came up the river in a wooden canoe, paddling themselves three miles from where they had been dropped by a river gunboat. Each man carried a small knife sharpened on both sides with a straight point and a .22 automatic pistol with a silencer attached.

They had memorized maps of the river and the layout of the huts and knew where their targets—they didn't think of them as men but as targets, didn't speak of them as men but as targets—were sleeping with their families.

The plan was simple. That was best. The very best plans were simple. Go into each hut, find the target by using an infrared light and special glasses they had brought, put two rounds in the head of each target, and then back into the canoe and down the river to the waiting patrol boat.

Simple.

They had done it before and they would probably do it again.

But an earlier visitor—a virus—had come to change things, change them dramatically. The virus had come in four days before, entered the children of the targets, and after four days of internal battling, the virus had won and the children had colds. They coughed and fretted and this night, the night the team was to hit, the children were at their worst.

The team could hear the coughing yards from the nearest tent. Then the soft voice of a woman comforting a child.

The team froze, waited for silence to resume, then made its way to the first target hut, where the coughing had been the worst.

They did not pause at the door to silhouette themselves, but stood to the side and rolled quickly in, using the light and glasses to locate the right sleeping pallet.

One of the team covered the rest of the sleepers and the other leaned down and fired twice into the temple of the sleeping target. The .22 made a sound like somebody clapping underwater and the target stiffened, the target's legs trembled, then the target became still.

They left the hut as they had come in, nobody awakened, no sounds.

In the second hut it was different. The team moved in, scanned with the infrared light and found the target, moved to the side of the target, and one of the team members leaned down to terminate, began to squeeze the trigger on the Colt Woodsman .22 automatic, when there was a sound.

The team functioned in darkness, silence. Any light, any sound was a threat to be dealt with, and the team member who was covering the security of the operation spun to handle the sound, spun and released two silenced rounds at the source of the sound to quiet it, to bring back the needed silence, while the first member of the team went ahead and terminated the target as they had terminated the first target. It was called sanctioning, the act of termination. When a target was *terminated, in the code of reporting it was said to have been sanctioned.*

The unexpected target to be sanctioned by the covering team member was a three-year-old child who had started to cough, would have coughed except that instinct and training took over and the two rounds went perfectly, exactly into the center of the child's head and forced it into silence and the child was sanctioned.

The first team member completed the termination of the target subject and turned to leave the hut and get back to the river and the boat and safety.

The covering team member stood, the .22 still raised, aimed at the spot where the child had sat up next to its mother before dropping to lie by her. Now there was other sound. The start of the child's cough had begun to awaken the mother; she stirred and her movement disturbed others in the room sleeping on mats.

Still the team member remained standing, frozen, his eyes wide and white.

"Come on," the first team member whispered. "We have to go!"

But the second team member couldn't make his feet operate. Nothing worked. He stared where the baby had been, stared where the bullets had gone, and stood.

"Damn it, Waylon, we have to move!"

"Leave me."

"No."

"Leave me, Wayne. Now. I'll stay here. It's better that I stay."

Wayne nodded, pretended to obey, and stepped closer, chopped once with the .22 pistol beneath Waylon's ear, up and hard and brutal, and Waylon was instantly unconscious and beginning to drop. Wayne caught him beneath the armpits, threw him up and over his shoulder in a fireman's carry, and ran out of the hut while people were sitting up, turning to see the bodies, before they could scream and react; out of the hamlet and down to the river and back into the darkness away from light, back into the silence.

The long silence.

WAYLON

5

He walked in beauty.

Wherever he went, no matter what was happening around him, to him, of him, he walked in beauty, in clouds of color, sprays of greens and blues and reds. He could see sunsets in a bus depot bathroom, hear Schubert in the roar of an engine, feel grace in a pile of mud.

Waylon Jackson.

He looked relatively normal for a forty-five-year-old child of the sixties and seventies. He was balding, with rounded shoulders that made him seem bearlike, strong arms, not fat but with a slight gut that pushed his jeans down and gave him a faintly redneck look. He kept his hair cut short on the sides, where he had hair, which enhanced the country look, and kept his beard short and even, or as even as he could hack it with scissors.

He washed his clothes regularly, worked when he needed money, had long before given up booze and drugs—which he'd tried in the seventies—and for thirty-two years had not had a place to live other than a room now and then, had not owned anything, and appeared on no forms except arrest blotters.

He was learning.

Now and then when he talked to people about himself—actually very rarely—and they asked him what he was doing and why, he would say, simply:

"I am learning."

And he meant it.

He tried to learn from every single thing he did or that happened to him or around him or of him. If asked he would say he learned from wars and flowers, weather and bugs, windows and rocks, sticks, cities, prisons, mountains, curbs, women, children, and liars.

"Everybody," he would say over his "furniture," "but politicians."

His "furniture" was a worn, loved, almost constantly used Martin twelve-string guitar that he carried in a beat-up leather case. It had been with him so long he didn't think of it as separate. When he dressed he put on his pants and shirt and shoes and picked up the guitar. He ate, drank, loved, and lived with the guitar next to him just as the music from the guitar was part of his breath, his life.

Sometimes he sang.

Throaty songs because his throat was old, but full, rich, earth tones that mixed with the bass chords on the guitar and stopped people when they tried to walk past him singing on the sidewalk; stopped them and made them throw money in his open guitar case and think of things like mothers they had never seen or loves they wished they had or dreams they hoped to have.

He walked in beauty, but he walked.

With the beauty, with the music in his head, the colors in his eyes and mind and soul, with the silver tinkling bells of his memories he walked; he lived, completely, for travel.

"You learn by moving," he said, and sometimes sang, for many things he thought and wanted to say came out in songs. "A stone is new if seen from the back; life floats in a moving stream and you have to move with it or it leaves you. . . ."

His travel took him to all places and all times. He'd been in race riots; hoed sugar beets with illegal Mexican workers; traveled down rivers with Pete Seeger; demonstrated against injustice; occupied university offices; been part of sit-ins, lay-ins, love-ins, stoned-ins; worn long collars and bell-bottoms and short hair, long hair, short hair, and finally almost no hair; tried to live with money, then without; married once for show, once in fear, and then, finally, not at all; did boycotts and strikes; rode the rails and jet airplanes; and at last, at the very last and yet the newest new part of his life, he'd come back to this:

Hitchhiking.

To stand on a road with a small cardboard sign that said in black felt-pen letters:

Will Sing for a Ride

Through the late eighties that way, through the messy, greedy, petty, vicious little late eighties, trying to get rides with a cardboard sign and facing the yuppies who stopped and tried to understand his anguish when he had none.

Will Sing for a Ride

And he would. Sing songs to them while he rode, sitting in the backseat, going nowhere, everywhere, no time, every time; sing songs of how ridiculous they were in their BMWs, sing songs of children starving while the yuppies wore their designer jeans and drank special water and spoke of gourmet wines and cultured yogurt and politically correct poetry. Not in anger, the songs, but in a kind of love and pity that they had become so shallow, so burned, so focused on self that the world had ceased to be important to them except for what they could print on a T-shirt.

Will Sing for a Ride

Across the country east to west and then north into Canada and back across west to east and twice more that way, singing and learning and hitchhiking until his songs had taken him to the edge of the middle.

The heart of it, close to the heart of it. Where food was grown by work to sing about, where steel had been made and fire tamed and freedom fought for; there, to stand there with the sign—the tenth sign, the hundredth sign. He had forgotten how many signs, how many towns, how many states, how many mountains. Forgotten everything but the people.

To stand with the sign:

Will Sing for a Ride

In Cleveland, Ohio.

THE RIDE

6

TERRY LOOKED SIDEWAYS at the car, kneeling down to make sure everything was even with the load on the luggage rack on the trunk lid. He could *not* think of it as a "boot."

He had packed his life, or so it seemed.

When he started he somehow didn't think of how far it was to go. But he found the road atlas in a corner of the closet and just looked at the distance across from Cleveland to Portland, Oregon, where the uncle lived, and it seemed another world.

He would be crossing most of the width of the United States. Except for a disastrous school trip on a bus that went to a museum in a town forty miles away— he couldn't even remember the name of the town—he had never been anywhere. All he saw on the trip was a

roomful of pioneer artifacts—for some reason he remembered a brass hand pump that went on a sink—and
a big kid named Richard Barris, who kept saying, "I'm
going to beat the hell out of you" to Terry for absolutely
no reason. Terry didn't even know the kid.

And now he was going to drive across the country.

When he went in to pack he was not logical. He took
a couple of T-shirts, an extra pair of pants, and some
socks. All this he crammed in a zipper bag he found in
his parents' closet, and for some reason at first he
thought that was all he would need.

Plus the money, of course. He took the money and
put some in each pocket, all the way around—he was
down to just over twelve hundred dollars now, what with
antifreeze and food—and was halfway to the garage door
with the bag, all set to leave, when he thought of a jacket.

He might get cold. There might be some cold
weather between Cleveland and Portland. He went back
for his windbreaker and then he saw a raincoat and
thought suddenly that the Cat didn't have a top. Of any
kind.

He needed some way to cover himself if it rained,
and that made him think of where he was going to sleep.
He couldn't just drive all the way through without sleeping, and that brought up camping, and if he was going
to camp he needed some kind of gear. . . .

Pretty soon he had half the house in the garage and
was trying to load it on and in the Cat. He had an old
tent he found in the garage along with a sleeping bag
and a large piece of plastic sheeting and a small camp
stove his father had used when he tried to take a fishing

trip that didn't come through as planned—a huge mound of stuff.

He shook his head, looking at the pile, and started over, loading each item carefully, thinking long on whether he would need it or not.

First his tools. He would probably need his tools. He put the whole four-drawer toolbox in the trunk, plus a canvas roll of screwdrivers and a tire tool and an old jack. The car had a small cheater-spare but it also had steel radials, so he hoped he wouldn't need it.

After the tools his clothes. Just enough for three days—he could stop at laundromats and wash. A jacket and a baseball cap and some wrap sunglasses to make him look older topped it off. He was tall and thin and the glasses gave him—he thought—a mysterious look and added at least five years to his life.

He took the plastic sheeting but left the tent. The sheeting was large enough to cover the whole cockpit and then some, and if it rained he could cover the car and sit inside and wait it out. He had never been camping in his life and didn't think this was a good time to start. At the last minute he threw in the sleeping bag.

He left everything else. Toys, models, a tired Nintendo, some comic books, junk he'd had since he was four.

The license plates posed a problem until he found a set. His father was always involved in one car deal or another and there was a set of car plates on the back of the workbench from one of his trades. According to the sticker the plates didn't expire for seven more months.

He put them on the car, figuring at least he didn't

look completely illegal now. He still didn't have a license, but there was a chance he wouldn't be stopped.

As for everything else—how to drive in traffic, what all the signs meant, how to handle different road conditions, everything would have to be learned as he went.

What was it they called it? He frowned, trying to think of what a teacher had said once about learning while you worked. *Oh yeah. On-the-job training.*

He would do on-the-job training to learn how to drive.

He started the Cat, listening to the engine a moment before backing out of the garage.

He stopped, left it running while he closed the garage door and returned, backed out into the street, and caught low and started forward.

It was already different, driving. Just going around the block, even with the steam boiling out of the cooling system, had given him a feel for the clutch and shifting. He was still a little rough, and he didn't use the brakes quite right, but it was smoothing fast and by the time he had driven eight more blocks and was near where he would get on the freeway heading west he had improved a hundred percent.

The Cat was a good teacher. It was responsive and tight and forgiving. If he oversteered, all he had to do was let the wheel go and it self-corrected, and though he sat low in the car he had enough visibility to see all around. It felt, he thought, like he was riding a four-wheeled motorcycle. He could hear and see things around the car as if he were out in the open.

The fuel gauge was wiggling between half and a quarter so Terry stopped at a small gas station to fill it up and check the oil and take a quick look at the engine.

"Nice car." A man came out of the station and looked at the Cat while Terry was filling the tank.

"Thank you." The gas cap was down on the side in the rear and it was hard to put gas in without dripping on the fiberglass.

"What kind is it?"

Terry shrugged. "I'm not sure what you call it. The name is Blakely Bearcat, but it's got all Ford parts. . . ."

"Oh. A kit car?"

"Yeah."

"Nice job. You build it?"

Terry nodded. And for the first time he felt proud of what he'd done. He liked the car and was happy building it, but there was something about having somebody else like it that made him feel proud.

The gas suddenly squirted back out of the hole as the cut-off on the pump worked. Apparently the filler tube was too narrow. He'd have to watch that in the future.

He paid and checked the oil again. It was still up and there didn't seem to be any oil leaks or steam from the antifreeze, so he clamped the hood down with the side hooks and started the car.

He looked both ways, jerked the clutch a little getting out into traffic, and accelerated until he got to the highway entrance, then downshifted and headed up the ramp onto I-40 heading west.

He was in traffic, moving west at sixty miles an hour, before he realized three basic problems.

First, it was getting dark and he had never really checked the headlights to see how they lined up.

Second, it was starting to rain. There were huge, gray clouds piling up and drops of water hitting the windshield.

Third, the car didn't have a top.

Somehow he always thought of riding in the sun. Didn't think of it raining when he wanted to drive, only at night when he was ready to stop.

He had the plastic sheet but he couldn't stop out here in the open, and even while he was thinking of it the rain was increasing.

Large drops were spattering across the windshield now and he turned the wipers on. There were three small wipers and he couldn't help smiling as they kicked in. They looked silly. But they worked.

He would have to hole up, take the next exit and pull the plastic out and wait for it to clear.

It was a mile and a half to the next exit and by the time he turned off the highway he was soaked.

He steered the Cat off the highway, down the exit ramp, and pulled over to the side at the bottom near some trees.

It took just a moment to pull the plastic out from behind the seat and spread it over the car, with him underneath, the water slithering off to the side. He left the engine running and flicked the switch for the heater. It was small, a little one-speed motor, but he felt warm air blowing onto his feet and thought it would help dry him off.

Dry or not, it was warm and he had not slept properly for over a week, just catching a doze when he could, and now with the heater blowing and filling the car with warm air, and the rain pattering on the plastic and the darkness coming down he could not keep his eyes open.

They closed gently and sleep started to take him, would have taken him except that on the passenger side of the Cat there was a rustling sound and a round face with a beard poked under the plastic.

"The quality of mercy is not strain'd;
   It droppeth as the gentle rain from heaven
      upon the place beneath.
   It is twice bless'd.
   It blesseth him that gives and him that takes."

And Terry opened his eyes for his first view of Waylon Jackson.

7

"WHAT . . . WHO?" Terry was only half awake.

"Shakespeare wrote that. It's about rain. I need mercy and a dry place to sit so I thought it was appropriate. Do you mind?"

Waylon slid in beneath the plastic, hunkering down. He left a backpack outside but brought in a guitar case—which barely fit down between his knees—and smiled over at Terry. "Cozy, isn't it?"

"I . . . didn't plan on company."

"Ahh, yes. A loner. I thought so. Me, too. But still, sometimes we have to work together or we fall apart, right?"

The guy is whacked, Terry thought. *Completely nuts. He's probably a serial killer. I'm sitting under a piece of plastic in the rain with a serial killer.*

But in some way he didn't feel afraid or threatened. The man looked friendly, crouched down, his face lighted by the glow from the instrument panel—Terry noticed that the light on the fuel indicator was flickering and he reached under the dash almost without thinking and pushed the light firmly into place—but still, he didn't want this guy sitting in the car. He didn't know him, didn't know anything about him.

"Clearly you're traveling. I noticed all the gear packed on the back luggage rack. Would you be going east or west?" Waylon asked.

"West," Terry answered promptly, then shook his head. "I mean I'm not sure." *I mean,* he thought, *it's none of your business,* but he didn't say it.

"Me, too. All the way to where the blue part starts. It's a long way to run alone, isn't it?"

Terry shook his head. "No, I don't mind. I do it all the time. . . ."

"Of course, of course. Still, a man gets lonely on such a long trip. And then, too, there's the expense. Gas, oil, breakdowns. Then there's the intellectual tedium."

Breakdowns, Terry thought. The possibility hadn't occurred to him. He had almost twelve hundred dollars left and it seemed like a lot of money. Still, if this man was willing to pay his way—he shook his head. He didn't know the guy. *Some weirdo gets in the car spouting Shakespeare and the next thing you know he kills you and chops you up and puts you in garbage sacks and mails the pieces to South America.* "Intellectual tedium?"

Waylon nodded. "It'll cause brain damage. That's what happened back in the fifties and then again all through the eighties. Tedium that led to brain damage. The whole damn world. You don't want that to happen to you, not driving across the country. You don't want to turn into something from the fifties or eighties— a lopped-out, intellectually dead piece of Republican manure—do you?"

"No." Terry shook his head, then shrugged. "I mean, I don't know. I guess not."

"Exactly. And I can keep that from happening."

"You can?"

"Absolutely. I've done it before. Many times."

"How?"

"It's complicated. There's music, and verse, and books, and just pointing at things. How old are you?"

Terry almost told him the truth, then caught himself and lied. "Eighteen."

Waylon studied him in the soft light, then nodded slowly. "I thought so—in fact I actually thought you might be nineteen."

"You did?" Terry asked hopefully.

"No. I'm lying there. You have to look for the lies— I'll be throwing them in from time to time. It helps to break the tedium. But you look older than your age, anyway. When I was your age I was on the road, except I didn't have a car. I thumbed it and rode some trains, worked here and there. Back in the early sixties . . ."

Terry frowned. "That was a long time ago."

"Was it?" Waylon smiled. "It seems like just last week sometimes." He lifted the plastic. "Look, the rain is stopping."

Terry lifted the plastic and peeked out into the darkness. A breath of warm, soft summer air hit his face and he pushed the plastic farther back. It had indeed stopped raining. A quick summer storm.

"Shall we go?" Waylon peeled his side of the plastic back all the way, pushing droplets of water down the side of the car onto the ground. He reached out and got his pack, held it in his lap.

And Terry thought of all the things he should say but didn't; thought of telling the man, Waylon, to get out, thought of telling Waylon that he wasn't really taking a trip but that his parents were waiting at home, but none of it came out.

"Right," he said. "West it is . . ."

The Cat was already running. He caught first, moved off the shoulder, crossed a small road, and caught second and third as the Cat nosed up the highway entrance back onto I-40.

Waylon shook the rest of the plastic off, folded it neatly, and put it down in the small opening behind the seats and leaned back, taking the summer night air on his face with the same soft smile he'd had earlier, when he first stuck his head in and spoke Shakespeare to Terry.

They moved onto the highway. Terry shifted the Cat to fourth and looked at the speedometer.

Sixty-five exactly. He had just seen a sign saying that was the speed limit. He didn't want to speed. If the cops stopped him they'd find out the plate wasn't really any good and that he didn't have a license and it would be all over. He'd have to take it easy.

But it was hard to think of problems.

He was heading west on a warm summer night. The stars were coming out. The headlights seemed to be adjusted about right. Waylon was humming some kind of tune next to him, and Terry didn't care about yesterday, tomorrow, last week, or next week.

Just tonight. And the road. And the car he'd made with his own hands.

The Cat.

8

THE HIGHWAY he took west—I-80/90—was a toll road. He went through the booth, feeling the man inside was staring at him, and then drove for two hours, holding sixty-five, letting the warm wind coming over the top of the windshield and around the sides blow Cleveland somewhere to the rear.

When he'd put the dashboard together it had come with a small map light that had given him problems. It hadn't fit the hole made for it, and he had finally used a round file to enlarge the hole. Then the wire in the harness that came with the kit hadn't been long enough and he had spliced a piece in to make it fit and the splice hadn't been good enough and now the light flickered.

He turned the light on and worked a hand up in the

area of the splice and squeezed it and the light glowed steadily.

Waylon was dozing, and Terry took a moment to study his face in the glow.

He seemed happy. Even sleeping he had a smile in his eyes somehow, some look that made Terry want to smile as well.

Terry was still concerned. He was setting out on a trip across the country with what amounted to a complete stranger. It was crazy. But the whole thing was crazy anyway. What was one more crazy part?

Waylon's eyes opened suddenly and he was looking directly into Terry's eyes. He smiled, or rather his sleeping smile widened.

"I have done this for so many years it all seems like one car, one highway, one country." He rubbed his face, looked at his wrist—there was no watch there but he nodded. "About three in the morning. This is the worst time to drive as far as sleep is concerned. You want me to drive awhile?"

Terry started. *Let somebody else drive the Cat?* "No . . . I'll take it."

"I thought as much. So then, we'll talk. What do you want to talk about?"

Terry shrugged. A truck moved past him on the highway and the wind from the trailer of the semi buffeted the Cat around. He held it in the center of the lane.

"How about how we should leave the highway?" Waylon asked.

"Why? It's good road and goes the direction we want to go and . . ."

"And it's patrolled heavily and you're underage, driving a car with invalid license plates, and if you get popped I get popped. It's not new for me. I was detained a few times back in the sixties and seventies—when getting arrested meant you cared. But it might not be so much fun for you."

"How did you know all that?" Terry had actually jerked the wheel in surprise at Waylon's words.

"I know you're underage because of how you look and how I see things. If you're too young to have a driver's license, the plates probably aren't valid. I know you haven't been arrested because we've met three state patrol cars and you didn't notice any of them. If you've ever been arrested you always see police."

"We did?" Terry turned and looked back. "Are they still around?"

"No. They were going the other way. But it might be a good idea to get off the toll road and travel the back highways. Toll roads suck."

"I kind of like them," Terry said. "They're so nice and wide."

"You don't see anything. Don't learn anything." Waylon put his arm out to the side and directed a stream of air against his face. "You don't learn, you die."

Terry said nothing, thought about what Waylon had said. A sign said there was an exit for a state highway in one mile. "How about that road? Will that take us where we want to go?"

"Where do you want to go?"

"West." Terry gestured with his chin. "To Portland, Oregon." He pointed across Waylon. "There's a small road atlas in that pocket on the door. Why don't you check on the map and see?"

Waylon nodded. "Take the exit, we'll work it out from there."

Terry turned off the toll road and came to a booth. He paid fifty cents and drove through—feeling this man was staring as well—and after a mile and a half pulled off onto a side road.

"What have you found?"

Waylon had the map under the little map light, tracing a line with his finger. "It goes for eight or ten miles and then turns into a county road, but if we cut west for twenty miles or so it becomes another state highway. Not a toll road. It all seems to work west."

Terry yawned. "I'm getting kind of tired."

Waylon nodded. "Maybe we better grab some sleep, and then I'll cook breakfast and we can get started on a full stomach. It's nicer to run in the day. You see more. You lea—"

"Learn more." Terry smiled. "I know."

"See?" Waylon leaned back in the seat and closed his eyes. "You're learning already."

Terry looked at him for a moment, then leaned back as well and closed his own eyes. In less than five seconds he was asleep.

9

THE SMELL awakened him; stole in over the door of the Cat, slid sideways and into his nose, and prompted a signal from his brain.

Food.

Food cooking.

Good food cooking.

Terry opened his eyes and found that he'd been sleeping with his head sideways over the seat, his mouth open. His neck was so stiff he couldn't straighten his head for a moment and he wiped drool from his chin.

Class, he thought. *I've got real class.* . . .

He had forgotten Waylon until his head popped up over the side of the car. "Morning. You ready to eat?"

That was the smell. Waylon was cooking.

"I have to pee," Terry said, "big time."

"Grab a bush."

Terry went to a nearby stand of willow, waited while a car passed before finishing, then came back to the car.

"You sleep good?"

"I think so. My neck is still bent."

"After a while you learn to keep your head straight."

Terry came around the rear end of the Cat and stopped.

There was what seemed to be a kitchen on the ground by the car door. Waylon had spread a small red-and-white checkered tablecloth and set it with two plastic cups, two metal plates—both dented but clean—and two forks and two knives. Off to the side a small camp stove with an external bright red aluminum tank was cooking quietly. On top of the stove was a one-gallon aluminum pot, also beat up but clean, and something in the pot was cooking with a smell that made Terry's mouth water. He suddenly remembered that he hadn't had a proper cooked meal in over a week—just bits of junk food while he worked on the Cat. Next to the pot but on the ground was a small coffeepot, also steaming.

"What is it?"

"In the small pot or the big one?"

"The big one."

Waylon smiled. "Beef stroganoff."

"What's that?"

"Beef and sour cream over noodles. Or it's supposed to be. I kind of make my own from a recipe I learned in Vietnam."

"What kind of recipe?"

"It's a can of beef stew on top of noodles with water and two tablespoons of nondairy creamer mixed in. Sit down and have some coffee—that's in the other pot. I'm sorry there aren't any napkins."

"Right." Terry squatted. "It ruins the whole thing, not having napkins."

I don't, he started to say, *drink coffee. But then I don't build cars or take off across the country, either. It might be time to try something new. It might be time to try everything new.* Besides, the smell of the coffee seemed to make his mouth water as much as the beef stroganoff.

Waylon poured coffee in both cups. It had cooled somewhat but was still hot enough to burn Terry's mouth when he took a sip. It tasted bitter.

"Is there sugar?" he asked.

Waylon shook his head. "Ruins it. Coffee has to be taken black or not at all."

Terry nodded but said nothing.

Waylon used a large spoon to ladle food from the pot onto the plates. "Eat up. We're wasting daylight."

Terry took a bite and found it to be hot as well as delicious. So good he kept trying to eat it hot, wiggling his tongue.

Waylon let his cool, then ate carefully, chewing each bite slowly, looking at the trees, the birds that flew past.

Terry finally got it all down and leaned back, belched. "That was incredible—where did you get it?"

"From my pack. I live in the pack."

"But a tablecloth? And two plates?"

Waylon cleaned his plate carefully, using a clump of grass. "It isn't necessary to be savage just because you aren't in a building." He pointed at Terry's plate. "That needs to be cleaned."

Terry nodded and used another clump of grass to clean his plate and fork.

"We'll use hot water on the plates when we stop for gas." Waylon put the eating equipment away, carefully fitting the pans and cups inside the cooking pot, then folding the tablecloth and placing it gently in the pack. When he was done, he tied the pack on top of Terry's bag on the back of the luggage rack and then pulled out the atlas. "Let's see where we're going."

Terry came around the car and looked at the atlas. "West," he said. "On back roads."

"Well, there's back roads, and then there's back roads." Waylon traced a finger on the map. "If we go this way, work these smaller state highways, we'll see some country but there's a chance we'll get stopped and we can't afford to get stopped, right?"

"Right."

Waylon studied Terry. "It isn't that you've done anything wrong, is it?"

Terry shook his head. "I don't think so. I just built the car and found the license plates in the garage to put on it."

"What about your parents?"

"They left me."

"Both of them?"

Terry nodded. "Sort of."

"Booze?"

Terry shook his head. "No. They just aren't the types who make parents."

"Are they going to be looking for you?"

Terry thought about it. "Maybe later. A lot later. In

two weeks or so. If they find I'm missing. But not right away."

"So we're just in a nonregistered vehicle."

"I guess so. Yeah."

"Which the police won't be looking for."

"I don't think so—why should they?"

"Well, if they're not looking for you and they're not looking for the car and they're not looking for me, we can take the better state roads and make some time. Let's do that, shall we?"

Terry was already back around the car and he dropped into the seat. "Just tell me where to go."

He turned the key and the starter cranked, but the car didn't start. He let it grind for a while, until the battery seemed to be wearing down, then stopped. "I don't know what's wrong."

"It cooled last night. She needs a little choke—just a minute." Waylon opened the hood and propped it on the rod braces, fumbled with the air cleaner on top of the carburetor, and removed it.

"Ahh, here. The choke isn't even hooked up." He worked the choke manually, held it closed. "Try it now."

Terry cranked the Cat again and it turned twice before firing off with a healthy roar.

Waylon smiled, let the engine warm before opening the choke and putting the air cleaner back on. He closed the hood and climbed into the car, holding his guitar in his lap again. "And away we go. . . ."

Terry made a mental note to fix up some kind of choke system, moved back onto the small highway, and headed west.

They drove steadily until almost eleven in the morning, then stopped for gas and to wash the breakfast dishes and buy more food because they'd used all the food in Waylon's pack. Waylon paid for everything—gas, food, a reserve quart of oil, though it didn't seem they'd need it because the Cat wasn't using any.

"You don't have to pay for everything," Terry said as they left the station. "I have some money. . . ."

"I'll buy. It's your car; you're driving."

Terry nodded, and the truth was, for the first time in his life he really *was* driving. He had been working at it since he'd started the day before, working at driving. And he had seemed to be doing it. The car moved forward, backward; he went fast, slow; he steered.

But through the morning he started to learn to *drive*. When they came to a corner on the narrow road—and there were many of them—he didn't just herd the car around the curve, he cornered it, decelerating on the way into the curve, keeping the nose of the Cat on the inside, shifting down if it was a sharp curve that slowed the car so the tachometer dropped below 2600 or so rpm, then powering out of the turn by accelerating until the next turn. He had read hot-rod books and car magazines since he was nine years old, had read about these things but didn't understand them fully until now; and they seemed to come to him naturally, as if he'd been doing them all his life.

He was completely lost in the driving, didn't care where they were going or where they had been, or how long it took to get there. All he cared about was the road and the sound of the engine and the small squeal from the tires when he made a turn correctly; and he learned on every turn, every downshift and upshift, every time he accelerated and felt the center of gravity shift.

He had wanted to try breaking the rear end loose ever since morning. In one of the hot-rod books he'd read they talked about popping the rear end loose and drifting on a corner until it lined up with the road coming out of the corner, and finally where the road went along a flat field—so he could see past the curve well ahead to make sure there was no traffic coming—he tried it.

Just as the car started to take the sideways pressure of the curve he jerked the emergency brake once, which stopped the rear wheels and they started to skid sideways, swinging the rear end around. At the same time he shifted down and when it was lined up on the road he powered out. It was rough, but it worked, and he kept a higher speed through the turn than he would have been able to hold driving normally.

Next to him he saw Waylon smile and nod.

"I never did that," Terry explained. "I thought it was a good place to try. . . ."

"You learn fast." He patted the dashboard of the Cat. "It's like one of the old MG-TDs. It even looks a little like one. Tighter, though, and flatter on the curves. People have lost this."

"Lost what?"

"How to drive, the art of driving. Now they get in technological monsters and barf around. They don't know how to drive, just be driven."

Terry nodded, though he didn't quite understand in

what way Waylon meant there was a difference between driving and being driven. He was going to ask, or at least talk more, opened his mouth to say something, when a dark shadow seemed to cover him from the side and the world blew up.

10

He nearly wet his pants.

Waylon was looking over his shoulder and his eyes went wide, then tightened at the corners and Terry turned.

There was a black Ford pickup next to him, painted in primer, flat black, and rocketing along on tires that seemed higher than the whole Cat.

It apparently didn't have mufflers, or if it did it had a cutout ahead of them. The noise was deafening, seemed to almost physically push at Terry as the truck roared alongside.

He looked up. In the right seat, looking down on him, was a man wearing a T-shirt with a cigarette pack rolled up tight in the sleeve. He had short hair, almost none, and he looked down on Terry and flipped his finger and spit.

They were doing about sixty and the wind took the spit away, but his meaning was clear. He turned and said something to the driver—Terry couldn't see across the truck to the driver—then reached over in the seat and came up with a beer bottle. The truck accelerated until it was slightly ahead of Terry and Waylon. The man held the bottle up to his mouth, took a swig, and held the bottle upside down, smiling crookedly.

"Kick it," Waylon said, yelling over the bellow of the truck. "Catch a gear and get out of here. *Now!*"

Terry floored the Cat and looked at the tach. They were near 3000 rpm now and it barely crawled forward; they were at too high a speed to accelerate without shifting down. If he dropped it a gear it would redline. He shook his head. "It'll blow the engine. . . ."

It was too late in any case. The man in the pickup flipped the bottle out of the truck window back at the Cat.

It seemed to come in slow motion, arcing back, and for a moment Terry thought it was coming straight at his head.

But at the last moment the bottle caught the steel top edge of the windshield and shattered back in Terry's face.

He had barely enough time to close his eyes before the glass hit him, and when it did reflex took over and he jerked the wheel of the Cat down to the right.

The Cat left the road at sixty, was airborne for three feet, then dropped into the ditch in a whipping sea of grass and dust.

"Damn . . ." Waylon reached for the wheel, trying to correct, but Terry had his eyes open almost at once and cut back to the left, then right, then left in decreasing swerves until the Cat came to a stop in the middle of the ditch, sitting on the grass.

The truck kept moving down the highway, and Waylon was out of the car almost before it stopped rolling and stepped around to Terry's side.

"Out."

The whole thing hadn't taken ten seconds. Terry got out of the car and Waylon bent him over frontward.

"Are your eyes clear?"

"I think so. Yeah."

"Brush all the glass out of your hair and off your clothing."

"What's the matter with those guys?"

"Drunk rednecks, freaks—who knows? There are people in the world who don't want to be part of the race." He looked down the road and his voice became quiet, almost a whisper. "There went two of them."

Terry cleaned his clothes, then they went through the car and made sure all the pieces of glass were out of the seats.

"Let's get it up on the road." Waylon moved around back. "You drive and I'll push."

Terry slid back into the seat and dropped it in low. Waylon didn't need to push. The ditch was dry and the wheels grabbed and they were back up on the road in a moment. Waylon got back in and pointed down the highway.

"Let's go."

Terry started, shifted to second, third, and fourth,

and then looked at Waylon. "This is the way those guys in the truck went."

Waylon didn't say anything but nodded.

"Maybe we should try to avoid them."

This time Waylon looked. "Why?"

"Because of what they did—they're dangerous."

Waylon smiled. "Not really."

Terry remembered the bottle crashing into the windshield frame. An inch higher and it could have killed him. That was dangerous enough.

They had been driving while talking and Terry saw a small farm town a mile or so ahead of them. He slowed. Somewhere he'd read that a lot of these towns were speed traps, or his dad had said it—it surprised him to think it because it was the first time he'd thought of his parents since he'd started, except when Waylon had asked about them—and he didn't want to get a ticket.

Closer he saw that there was a gas station on the outside edge of town.

Still closer he saw that the black truck was in the gas station. He let the Cat slow.

Waylon had seen the truck as well and he motioned toward it. "Let's stop for gas."

"What?"

"You need gas." Waylon pushed his guitar off to the side and unbuckled his seat belt. "Stop."

Terry looked at the VDO gas gauge. It was still at three-quarters full. "We don't need gas."

"Yes." Waylon looked at him, his eyes serious. "We do. Stop there."

This is insane—just looking for it, Terry thought, but there was something in Waylon's eyes, some force he did not understand, and without meaning to he slowed and brought the Cat up to the gas pumps.

"You pump," Waylon said, sliding out of the car. "I'll pay."

Right, Terry thought, *I'll pump*. He shook his head. *If you think I'm going to stay out here while you're in there. . . .*

He left the car and followed, as it worked out, eight or ten steps behind Waylon. Waylon opened the front screen door to the gas station and walked inside like he didn't have a concern in the world.

Terry stopped at the door, holding it open. He could see the inside because of light coming through a back window. There was a counter down the right side of the room with a cash register on top of it near the front door. Two men stood next to the counter, one drinking a Bud, the other smoking a cigarette. Terry recognized the one smoking as the guy in the truck who had thrown the beer bottle. Another man, the owner or somebody who worked at the station, was in back of the counter drinking a Coke. It was clear the three were friends, were talking and laughing—probably about the beer bottle and the Cat.

Too many, Terry thought. *There are three of them. One of them is too many. Three is an army. Don't—don't do this.* But none of it came out. He just watched.

Waylon walked down along the counter, his arms swinging loosely at his sides.

"Well, look at this," the man with the cigarette said. "It's them we were just telling you about—from the little kiddy car." He stood away from the counter and faced Waylon. "Are you a couple of little kiddies?"

Waylon stopped. Terry could not see his face but his voice sounded soft, almost sad.

"It can go either way," Waylon said. "It's up to you. You can make it rough or you can make it easy. The point is you could have really hurt the boy. I think you should apologize and we'll call it square."

"Apologize? Hell, I missed him, didn't I? What more do you want?"

Terry did not see exactly what happened next. Waylon seemed to move, a shrug that took his whole body, and there was a chunking sound, like meat being dropped on a counter, and the man went down holding his throat, blood running out of his nose and mouth.

Waylon took a step forward, shrugged once more, and the second man from the truck went down as well. He was holding his knee and also bleeding from the nose and mouth.

Waylon looked at the man who owned the garage, who was still standing in back of the counter, a bottle of soda halfway to his mouth. Not four seconds had passed since Waylon had first shrugged.

"I wasn't part of it," the station owner said, raising his hands and waving them. "Looks like they had it coming."

Waylon nodded, moved back to where Terry stood by the door. "You didn't get any gas, did you?"

Terry shook his head. "What did you do to them?"

Waylon didn't answer, instead guided Terry out of the door and back to the car.

"I didn't even see you touch them," Terry said, following. "You just shrugged or something and they went down—how did you do that?"

But Waylon didn't speak and continued to not say anything even when they were on the road and moving at sixty-five.

He sat staring ahead while Terry drove. Not saying anything, not smiling, not singing or whistling, just staring and sometimes shaking his head.

Finally, just before dark, he looked at the atlas and leaned across the car. "We'll keep going tonight, drive all night. I'll take over when you get tired."

"But . . ."

"We need some work done on the car. And me. What I did back there was wrong. We need to get to Omaha tomorrow. To fix things. Just keep driving."

Terry nodded.

The light dimmed and he turned on the headlights, aimed the Cat west, and let it roll, following the sunset.

11

TERRY OPENED HIS EYES into bright light.

It was morning, early, and the Cat was burbling along. He had been sleeping with his head straight back against the seat and he sat up to see Waylon driving with a new sun at his back.

He hadn't wanted to let Waylon drive. The Cat was his, a part of him. He had tried to drive himself and had done all right until midnight. But then between midnight and one in the morning a switch had gone off somewhere in his head and it seemed everything shut down. He had tried to stay awake, fought it as hard as he could, but his chin kept dropping and finally he had pulled to the side of the road and let Waylon take over.

Perversely, as soon as Waylon started to drive, Terry snapped awake and for half an hour couldn't sleep. He watched Waylon drive and felt like he'd given his life away.

But Waylon was a good driver, shifted nicely on the power curve and kept the car moving right, and soon Terry had dropped off again.

Until now.

"Where are we?" he asked, squirming in the seat to get a good view. The sky was clear except for a couple of strips of white high cirrus, blue and starting to get hot.

"About twenty miles out of Omaha. Can you wait until we get there to stop or do you want me to pull over now?"

"I'm all right."

"There's some coffee in a thermos under your feet. It's hot and I put some sugar in it for energy."

"Thermos? I didn't know you had a thermos."

Waylon nodded. "I didn't have one. We stopped for gas in the night and I bought one at a truck stop. Filled it, figuring we would want some later."

Terry shook his head. "And I didn't wake up?"

Waylon laughed. "Not a flicker. You were really zonked."

Terry poured coffee. He had never liked it, and still didn't, but there was something about it that went with the morning, and he sipped contentedly.

"You want to drive?" Waylon asked.

"I'll take it later, after we get . . . Where are we going, anyway?"

"An old friend named Wayne Holtz. He lives this side of Omaha, ten or twelve more miles. He knows a lot about cars and about me—we both need fixing."

"I don't know what you mean." Terry shrugged. "I think the Cat is all right—it runs good, doesn't it?"

"It's great. But it could use a little more . . . just a little more. That's what Wayne does. Makes things work a little better."

"And you don't seem broken. Those guys didn't touch you, as far as I could see."

Waylon shook his head. "It's not physical. I shouldn't have done that to them. They were just a couple of good old boys getting drunk."

"They threw a bottle at me."

"At the car," Waylon corrected. "Just being stupid. I . . . hit . . . them wrong. The wrong way. One of them won't ever be right again." He trailed off, grew quiet, then smiled sadly. "We'll talk to Wayne a couple of days, work on the car, smooth the world out a little."

For a few minutes they moved in silence except for the wind coming over and around the windshield. Terry heard a meadowlark singing as they passed a fence post, a whip of sound, high and beautiful and gone before it really registered, and then Waylon was slowing.

"Along here, somewhere. Look for a metal sign cut in the shape of an artist's palette. . . ."

"A what?"

"A palette—what they mix paint on. . . . Ahh, there, see it?"

Terry caught a glimpse of a funny oblong metal sign with dabs of color around the outside edge and the word *ART* directly in the center. It seemed to be faded a bit, but they were past it too fast for him to tell anything else about it.

Waylon steered off the highway down a gravel road

for a mile or so, then off that road onto a quarter-mile-long driveway, and as they came to the end of the drive-way, around a bend and past some trees, Terry saw a large metal building. It was rusty and run down. Next to it stood an old trailer house, also run down and tired-looking, and everywhere else, or so it seemed, there were parts of cars and motorcycles rusting away.

"It's a junkyard," Terry said.

Waylon shook his head. "No. It's a place to create things. Come on."

The metal building had a large front door and a smaller door to the side. Waylon entered the side door without knocking and Terry followed, expecting it to be dark inside.

Instead the walls and ceiling were painted flat white and large floodlights lit the center so brightly Terry squinted and had to close his eyes.

He opened them to see a woman standing on a small platform, leaning against a tall stool with her arm across it, facing him full on.

She was completely, absolutely stark naked.

"Unnnhhh." Terry stopped dead and thought he should turn, knew he should turn, at least close his eyes.

He could do none of those things. He stood and stared. She was the most beautiful woman he'd ever seen, more beautiful than pictures in the magazines he had under his mattress at home. And there she stood. Wearing air.

The woman ignored him, and Waylon. Did not move. To the side a man who looked like he was completely made of hair and wearing only a pair of impossibly torn Levi's had an easel set up with a large canvas on it. There was a painting of the woman on the canvas, and the man turned as Waylon came in.

"Waaiiilll-*on!*" he yelled. He dropped the brush on a shelf on the easel and grabbed Waylon and hugged him. "How in hell *are* you? I heard you was dead. They said a train killed you, but I knew that was a lie. It would take more than a train. . . ."

"It was another guy. I was next to him when the train hit him and they thought it got us both. You know how rumors are."

"Right, right." Wayne suddenly seemed to notice Terry. "Who's your friend?"

"A traveling companion, name of Terry. He picked me up two nights ago and we've had a little trouble and need some help with his car."

"That's what I *do*. . . ."

Terry was still standing, staring at the woman, and Waylon laughed and spoke to her.

"Maybe you'd better put some clothes on, Suze—I think you're hurting his brain."

The model nodded but didn't move until Wayne motioned with his chin. "We'll stop for the day. We've worked enough—now it's time to *play*."

The woman stepped down from the stand, moving as naturally as a soft wind—or so it seemed to Terry— and put a housecoat on, and at last Terry could take his eyes away from her.

It was the first time since he'd come in the room that he could look around, and he saw now that on all the walls, hanging from wire hooks, there were gas tanks from motorcycles and parts of car hoods or air scoops and on most of them were paintings of nude women with large breasts in various poses. Here and there, there was a tank painted with an eagle or a skull and crossbones but most of them were women.

Wayne wiped his hands on a rag and washed his brushes in a sink near one wall, and Terry realized that he lived in this same building. There was a bathroom in a back corner—the only closed-in room—and a large bed off to the right side of the building.

"What's with the car?" Wayne asked, when he'd finished the brushes.

"It's outside. A home-built. It's fine, but we need a little more punch."

"We'll look at it. Suze—" He turned to the woman, who had moved to a chair under a lamp by the bed and opened a book. "Why don't you start some dinner while we look at the car?"

She looked up, directly at Wayne, and Terry saw in the light that her eyes were purple, and he realized with a start that she was the one not just on the canvas but on almost every gas tank.

"You mean me?" she asked. "You want *me* to cook?"

Wayne frowned, then shook his head. "I guess not."

"I don't cook. You know that. And I don't clean. I model and you pay me."

"Right."

"You'd better get your brain checked," she said, going back to the book. "Even asking is crazy."

Wayne turned and went out the front door and stopped outside in front of the car.

"Oh wow, man. It's a Blakely Bearcat!"

"You know the car?" Waylon moved off the side and Terry stood by the car.

"Know it? I helped a guy build one once. A guy named Blakely wanted Ford to build them and sell them, back in the late seventies. He made about four hundred of them and sold them as factory makes. Then Ford said no and he started selling them as kits. They rod up real good, real good." He turned to Terry. "What's it got inside?"

"A 1974 Ford Pinto motor."

"That twenty-three hundred-cc mill?"

"Yes—that's what it said."

"Oh, man, you guys are in luck."

"What do you mean?" Waylon asked.

"That's a hell of an engine—incredible. With just a few modifications we can increase the power seven or eight percent, but that ain't the best."

Waylon had let himself slide down the wall and was sitting in the dirt, smiling peacefully. His smile widened. "What else?"

"I got a blower for it."

"A turbocharger?"

Wayne nodded. "Some guy left it here in a box to pay for his Harley. It's made by a company out in California—Bunks or something. The thing drops right in where the exhaust manifold goes, clean as snot."

"A turbocharger?" Terry's ears perked. "What's that?" He had heard about them but didn't quite understand how they worked.

"It's a high-speed fan that drives from the exhaust gases and pushes accelerated air into the carburetor. It's like everything feeds on itself, man. The faster you go, the more air gets pushed, the faster you go." Wayne was so excited he was hopping around. "We can do it all in a day, max."

"Does it really make a difference?"

Wayne stopped, stared. "A *turbo?* How about night and day? It will increase your engine power by up to forty-five percent—you won't even know the car when we're done."

Terry stood, one hand on the car, and shook his head. "I don't know. How expensive is it?"

"Like new the turbo is a couple grand. But I can let you have it for . . ." Wayne hesitated and looked out of the corner of his eye at Waylon, who shook his head. "I can barter it off. You help me clean the place up and I'll put it in the car for you. Better yet, you help me put it in the car and we'll call it square."

Terry looked at Waylon, at Wayne, started to say something, and stopped. How long? Three days—he'd been with Waylon three days and now he'd just met a man who was going to give him a turbo, seen a naked woman with violet eyes, and watched a fight he still didn't understand. He sighed. "Thank you. But I think I should pay something."

Wayne shook his head. "No way, José. . . ."

"Later. When I'm rich I'll send you some money," Terry said.

Wayne smiled. "Right on. When you're rich. Now let's get to work. We've got to get the car inside and pull the exhaust system."

He went back in the side door and Terry heard chains rattling and the large door went up six feet. Terry started the Cat and pulled it in, and within moments he and Wayne were under the hood, loosening the exhaust manifold and the tailpipe assembly, the two of them working as hard as Terry had worked alone.

It grew dark but it didn't matter. The interior floodlights of the building were brighter than daylight.

Suze sat reading for a long time—Terry saw the cover of the book once and it said *Kafka* in large letters—then relented and got up and went to the refrigerator and made sandwiches with turkey and lettuce and mayo. Terry and Wayne ate with greasy hands, ripping into the car, but Waylon didn't eat.

He sat outside, watching the night come down, leaning against the wall, his eyes open but not seeing, a small frown on his forehead.

Hour after hour they worked, and once when Terry went outside to stretch his back he saw that Waylon was still sitting there, quietly looking into the night.

"What's the matter with him?" Terry asked Wayne when he came back inside.

"Nothing. He needs to think."

"About what?"

"About himself. He'll be in when he settles some things. Hand me that nine-sixteenths box and open end, will you?"

"Can we help him?"

Wayne looked out the door. "Did he go against someone?"

"You mean fight?" Terry nodded. "There were some guys in a pickup who threw a bottle at us. He made me stop at a garage and he did something to them. It wasn't really fighting."

Wayne turned back, sighed. "They went down, right?"

Terry nodded. "I was worried. I thought, you know, because he was so old they would hurt him. . . ."

"Old—who? Waylon?"

"Well, you know. Kind of old."

Wayne snorted and Terry thought it might have been a laugh but wasn't sure. "Old doesn't mean bad. It isn't age, it's where your head is at. And let me tell you something—where Waylon's head is at is a very, very hard place. Hard and cold and lonely." He shook his head. "Those guys are lucky he didn't terminate them."

"Terminate? You mean *kill?*"

But Wayne was back at work on the motor and didn't answer, worked in silence while Terry helped him and looked outside at Waylon sitting on the ground, leaning back against the building, looking at the sky.

"How long have you known him?"

Wayne glanced up and out at Waylon. "Oh, we go back a long ways. Did a little war, a little peace together. There was a time when he thought he was in love with me, but I ran off with a girl named Carmelita, had black hair that hung down to her ankles and could sing. . . ."

"Love? You mean, like, if he was gay or something?"

Wayne nodded and went back to work. "Yeah. He's gay. You didn't know?"

Terry stared at Waylon. "But he never . . . I mean, we've been together three days and he hasn't . . . You know . . ."

Wayne put his wrench down and studied Terry. "Made a move on you? Hell, boy, he's gay, he's not a pervert. You're just a kid, why would he make a move on you?"

"Well . . ." And the truth was Terry couldn't think of an answer, nor did it seem important. He shrugged and went back to work on the engine with Wayne.

12

"You ready to test her?"

Wayne stood over the engine, his hands and head covered with grease—where they weren't hidden by his hair—his smile a cut of white across the dirty face.

Terry was across the Cat, one hand on the windshield. It was early morning. They had worked all night—Terry thought he would never sleep correctly again—and the turbocharger was in place, shining and new-looking though it had been in the box for perhaps years. It was simple in concept. The exhaust manifold had been removed and replaced with the turbo. When the engine fired, the exhaust gases were expelled through the turbo, which was in reality a fan with a duct that led back to the carburetor. When the engine ran, the expelled gases turned the fan and that drove high-pressure air into the carburetor, which dramatically increased the power.

Or, Terry thought, it was supposed to. But he had never seen anything work this way and most of what had been done was accomplished by Wayne who was—as far as Terry could tell—the best mechanic in the world, or near it. Except that he just worked and didn't say what he was doing, so much of it was still mysterious to Terry.

But he nodded.

"Well, get in—crank her."

Terry slid into the seat and held his breath, turned the key, pushed it over to start.

There was a moment's hesitation and then the engine fired with a snort and a thundering growl. The Cat was just outside the door of the garage, but the sound was so deafening that Suze ran from the trailer to close the garage door and protect herself.

"It's loud," Terry said, or yelled, smiling at the same time. It sounded like he thought a car should sound—hungry.

Wayne nodded, leaned over, and yelled back. "That's because we dropped the muffler and put in that swollen piece of pipe to make it reverb a little. The muffler created too much backdraft for the turbo. Rev her a few times."

Terry pushed on the accelerator once, twice, and the sound grew, roared, filled the world. "Wow . . ."

Wayne nodded. "Far out, right? Oh, man, I can dig this thing. Let's go for a ride, see how it works."

Terry waited while Wayne got in. Waylon was nowhere to be seen and Terry supposed he had gone into the trailer to get some sleep.

Wayne closed the door. "You've got to watch it. It will seem the same for the first second or so, but the turbo kicks in fast and she can get squirrelly."

Terry nodded, put the Cat in reverse, turned around to look over the back, and eased the clutch out. It was loud but didn't seem much different.

"You don't want to give her too much—," Wayne started to say.

But he was too late. The Cat seemed unchanged to Terry and he pushed on the acclerator.

A pause, half a beat, then the turbo started pushing air, mixed it under pressure with the gas in the carbu- retor, and forced it into the pistons.

Both back tires broke loose.

There was a screech that nearly broke eardrums and the Cat was suddenly doing thirty-five miles an hour. In reverse.

"—gas," Wayne finished, his head snapping forward with the acceleration.

Terry instinctively cranked the wheel to the right, the car swerved flatly back to the left, whipped around, and he was looking down the driveway over the front end. He clutched, shifted into low, accelerated again, and they were aimed at the road doing almost fifty—all in the space of two or three seconds.

On the road he caught third, brought her up to sixty, then fourth, and pushed the accelerator where it would have been previously for seventy.

The Cat jumped to just under a hundred miles an hour and when he backed down to where it would have been for normal cruising speed there was over half the pedal still left.

"Wow . . ." He shot a quick look at Wayne. "This is incredible."

"Far out, right? I dig your driving. Man, that turn in the driveway was pure Sterling Moss."

Terry had slowed to turn around at a wide place in the road. "Who's Sterling Moss?"

Wayne stared at him. "You don't know the name?"

Terry shook his head. "Never heard of him. Did he drive or something?"

"Oh, man. Never heard of Sterling Moss. Oh, this is too much. Sterling Moss was the driver, *the* driver back in the sixties and seventies—there were people who said his name would live forever when he won the Grand Prix. He could take turns like nobody has ever taken turns. It looked like his inside wheels were bolted to the road—and you don't know him. Oh, man, that crushes. That really crushes."

While Wayne was talking, Terry had turned and driven back to the driveway and was now pulling up to the metal building. Waylon came outside when they arrived, drinking a Coke and eating a sandwich.

He and Wayne looked at each other—Terry caught the look—and Waylon nodded, almost imperceptibly, and Wayne answered the nod. Then he waved a hand toward Terry.

"He doesn't know who Sterling Moss was."

Waylon shook his head. "Tragic." But he was smiling softly.

"Well, dammit, think of it. He loves cars, drives like he was born to it, and doesn't know Sterling Moss. How can that be?"

Waylon took a sip of Coke. "So he never learned about Moss."

"Exactly. My point exactly. He never learned." Wayne took a breath. "The question is, my friend, how much other stuff doesn't he know?"

Waylon nodded slowly.

"You know what I think?" Wayne stood, his hand still waving toward Terry.

"No. What do you think?" Waylon burped.

"I think we should find out what he doesn't know. There might be a shocking lack of fundamental knowledge here."

All this time Terry had been sitting in the car, one hand draped over the wheel, the motor turned off. "How can you do that? I don't know what I don't know."

Wayne turned. "Simple. We'll ask until we hit a blank. Let's start with . . . Hell, I don't know. Waylon, what should we start with?"

Waylon had picked up his guitar, which had been resting against the wall at the side of the door, and tickled the strings, making a sound like rain.

"Music. Let's ask about music."

Wayne nodded, turned to Terry. "What do you know about music?"

Terry shrugged. "I don't know. I listen to it. I like some of it."

"No." Waylon hit a stronger chord. "Not the sound, the groups. The writers. The composers."

"Dylan," Wayne said, raising a hand. "Bob Dylan."

Terry frowned. "No—I don't know him."

"You don't know Bob Dylan?" Waylon moved toward the car. "How about Pete Seeger?"

Terry snapped his fingers. "Bob Seger. I've heard of him."

"But not Pete?"

Terry shook his head. "Nope. Sorry."

"Different Seegers," Wayne said. "Way different."

"Ian and Sylvia?" Waylon asked. "Bud and Travis? Elvis?"

"I know Elvis. Of course."

"And the Beatles?"

"I know of them. I've seen them on old videos."

Wayne stopped them. "I think we've got a base here. He pretty much doesn't know anything about music before maybe 1980 or 1985, except for Elvis and the Beatles."

Waylon nodded. "I think you've got it."

"Which," Wayne said, "is the same as not knowing anything."

"How about Bruce Springsteen?" Terry asked. "I heard him once. . . ."

Wayne shook his head. "Not real. He came late. Nobody who was anybody listened to him."

"Move into rock a little," Waylon said, "Jimi Hendrix, Jefferson Airplane, Grace Slick . . ."

Terry sighed. "Nope."

". . . Simon and Garfunkel?"

"Nope."

"God." Wayne wiped his face. "It's like he wasn't born or something."

"I wasn't," Terry pointed out. "They were all before I was born."

"Well, there you are." Wayne nodded. "That explains it. You weren't around."

"Books," Waylon said. "What books have you read?"

"The ones I have to, for school."

"Any Steinbeck—*Grapes of Wrath, Tortilla Flats?*"

"Nope. I watched part of a movie called *Grapes of Wrath* on television, but it was pretty boring."

"Boring . . ."

"Yeah. About a bunch of farmers and they get into a lot of dust or dirt or something. Is that it?"

Waylon turned away, struck another chord, then back. "That's the right story, but the wrong way to see it, to know it."

"*Don Quixote,*" Wayne said, leaning over the car. "About a Spanish guy who ran around sticking spears in windmills?"

Terry held up his hands. "Sorry. I've never heard of it."

"History," Waylon said suddenly. "Let's try history. Washington, Jefferson . . ."

Terry brightened. "I've heard of them. Of course."

"What have you heard?"

"Well, like that Washington won the Revolutionary War and Jefferson wrote the Declaration of Independence, and they were both presidents."

"But other than that—about the men?"

"Well, I guess not much."

"That Washington became very wealthy by swindling his own soldiers out of land and had wooden teeth and many slaves, or that Jefferson died in virtual bankruptcy—you've never heard that?"

"No."

"The Civil War."

Terry leaned back. "I can't think of anything. You know. Right off the top."

"The West."

"Cowboys, Indians, like that?"

"Yes."

"Well, just that. I've seen old movies. . . ."

"But no reading about it."

"No."

For a minute, a full minute, there was silence. Terry heard a bird song that seemed to match the chords Waylon had been picking. Then another half a minute passed, nobody saying anything until Wayne coughed.

"America—he needs to find America."

Waylon looked at him and slowly nodded.

"That's what he needs. To go and see it and find it." Wayne pushed. "Like we did—you know, after the war."

"After the war," Waylon repeated.

"Yeah. You got to go trucking."

"Trucking?" Terry cut in. "I don't know anything about trucking."

"No," Wayne stopped him. "That's what we used to call it—traveling. We went trucking. That's what you need to do. Go see America. Truck on out."

"No," Waylon said, turning to put his guitar back in the case. "It's what *we* need to do. *We* need to go trucking."

"We?"

"Yeah. You've got to come with us. We've got to go find it again. You take Baby."

Wayne looked at Waylon, studied his eyes, then looked down at Terry and back up and grinned. "Yeah—

you're right. We've got to go find it again, man. See if it's still there. Right on. It's time for me and Baby to ride."

Terry sat in the car, looking up at the two men, wondering what they were doing to his life.

"Who," he asked, "is Baby?"

13

BABY was a Harley.

Or, as Waylon pointed out later, Baby was *the* Harley.

It is possible that of all the Harley Davidson motorcycles owned by all the Harley owners who loved their bikes—and many of them took them into their homes at night, named them, talked to them—there was never a Harley as pampered and loved as Baby.

Wayne left them and moved back into the metal building and went to a small secondary room at the back that Terry had seen before but assumed was a storage room for paint or materials.

It was for Baby.

Wayne opened a door on the side of the room and

disappeared inside and came out a moment later wheeling Baby.

Terry climbed out of the Cat to get a better look. It was turquoise-green and white, with a slight rake to the front fork—although not as excessive as he had seen on some bikes—and every square inch, every nut and chrome-plated cover or bolt, or fender or the twin tanks, was absolutely spotless. Even the black leather saddlebags were clean, smooth. Baby shone in the morning sun, seemed to emanate a light of its own.

"It's beautiful," Terry said. "Really beautiful."

Wayne smiled. "Thanks. I spend a little time on her."

Suze came into the building from the trailer, wearing a long sweatshirt and holding four cups of steaming coffee. She handed one to Waylon, another to Terry, and held Wayne's until he put the kickstand down on the bike and could take it.

"You going?" she asked sleepily, sipping her coffee.

Wayne nodded. "You handle things while I'm gone?"

She shrugged. "Depends on how long."

"Until we get back. We're going to look at some things. See a little country."

"Write if you get work." Her voice was tough sounding, but she reached out a hand and patted Wayne softly on the cheek, and Terry felt they had done this before, maybe many times.

Terry took a sip of his own coffee, found she had put sugar in it, and realized with the first taste he was starving. He hadn't eaten since the sandwich the day before and his stomach grumbled when the coffee hit bottom.

"We'll eat after we leave," Waylon said. He had moved to stand next to Terry and heard his stomach. "On the way . . ."

Wayne went to the side of the building and pulled down an old duffel bag stuffed with gear.

"My trucking bag," he said, and used elastic bungee cords to affix it vertically to the sissy bar on the seat. Then he straddled the bike and smiled. "You guys ready?"

Like that, Terry thought—*that fast he could leave?* And remembered his own leaving, all the gear he had tried to take, and Wayne just flipped the duffel bag onto the bike and was ready to go.

Waylon put his own pack on the back of the Cat and nodded at Terry. "You ready?"

Terry nodded. "I think so."

Waylon started to get in and then stopped, his hand on the door.

"What's the matter?" Wayne had turned the gas and key on the Harley and paused.

"Legal problem. He's working on illegal plates. We could get stopped."

Wayne smiled. "No-o-o problem. We'll stop on the way out and register the car in my name, get plates, and we're on our way."

But . . . , Terry thought. *But doesn't that mean you own the Cat? On paper, legal and all?* Except that he didn't say it, couldn't say it. Wayne had pushed the starter button on Baby and the tuned pipes rattled and roared and it was impossible to say anything.

With another look at Suze, and a small nod from her, Wayne popped the bike into gear and slid around the Cat and out into the morning, down the driveway and out to the road.

Waylon dropped into the seat and closed the door. "Follow," he said, waving his arm backward, "the bouncing bike."

And they were on their way.

14

THEY DIDN'T head west out of Omaha.

It was early morning and Terry followed Wayne while he went to the courthouse, took the title papers from Terry, and went inside. Twenty minutes later he came out with license plates. They put them on the Cat, and Wayne took a pen from his saddlebags and signed the place on the title that transferred ownership.

"All you do is keep the title in my name. When you're ready to change it—you know, later—you sign your name on it and take it into the courthouse where you live and they'll transfer the title back to you . . . ," he trailed off, looked at Waylon. "North all right?"

Waylon nodded and Wayne fired the Harley up and they moved down side streets until they came to a highway heading north of Omaha before noon.

Still, Terry noted, without eating.

It was a beautiful day, however—hungry or not—and nice to be moving, the wind whipping around the cockpit while they followed Wayne on the Harley.

"Hungry?" Waylon asked when they were well clear of the city.

Terry nodded. "I could eat road kill."

"Just a minute." Wayne turned and rummaged in a side pocket of his pack and came up with a package of trail mix. Terry hated trail mix—it made him feel like he was eating dry cereal with no sugar-milk on it—but he took some that Waylon poured in his hand and munched it.

It tasted delicious. Almost sweet. But there was too little of it and Waylon had put the bag back in his pack.

"Can we have more?" Terry pointed at the pack with his thumb. "I'm still hungry."

He was surprised to see Waylon shake his head. "You want to stay hungry—from here on you want to stay hungry."

Terry pulled out to pass a truck. "I do? Why?"

"To learn," Waylon said. "You always stay hungry to learn. You get full, you get sleepy, lazy; you get lazy, you don't learn."

"What are we going to learn driving on a highway?"

Waylon laughed. "Anything you want to know."

"But what?"

"That's the question, isn't it? What do you want to know?"

"I don't know. . . ."

Waylon peered at him, then back out the windshield. "I don't believe it—there's nothing you want to know?"

"Well, sure, lots of things. But I can't think of them now."

"Not one thing?"

Terry frowned. "Well, all right. Why are we heading north? I thought we were going to go west."

"We're heading north because Wayne is heading north and we're following him."

"Why is he heading north?"

Waylon shrugged. "I guess there's something he wants to know up north."

"What?"

"I don't know. We'll follow him and find out. That's how you truck. You don't necessarily get anywhere, you just go. . . ."

And go they did. Wayne kept the northern pace for almost two hours, over a hundred miles, before stopping for gas. They were just past Sioux City, Iowa, when they stopped.

Terry filled the Cat while Wayne gently put gas in Baby, then walked over while Waylon paid—he still wouldn't let Terry pay.

"Why are we heading north?" Terry asked.

"Because that's where Samuel is," Wayne said. His hair had been in the open wind all the while—there was no windshield on Baby—and both his hair and beard were blown back and stuck full of bugs.

"Who is Samuel?"

"Samuel is somebody you have to meet if you want to understand America. He's far out."

Waylon came out then with Cokes for all three of them and a package of doughnuts. They stood by the pumps and the car and bike, eating doughnuts and drinking Coke. Terry could feel the sugar tear into him, but when he'd had only one doughnut Waylon closed the sack and put it in the car. "Enough."

They headed out again. Once they were in traffic and the Cat was up to speed in back of the Harley, Waylon leaned over.

"You find out why we're heading north? I figured you'd ask."

Terry shrugged. "He wants me to meet somebody named Samuel. Who is Samuel?"

Waylon smiled. "Samuel is somebody you have to meet if . . ."

". . . I want to learn about America. Yeah, he said that, too."

"Far out," Waylon said, smiling.

"And he said that, too."

"Right on—we'll go until dark and then camp. Drive on, Macduff. . . ."

Camping was more formalized with Wayne along.

Darkness caught them at a campground just out of Yankton, South Dakota, down along a river under tall elms. The campground was deserted except for one pickup camper with a couple that sat inside watching television on a small set that made a blue-gray glow out the windows of the camper.

Waylon was ready to just pull the tarp up and sleep in the car, as they'd done the first night out, but Wayne shook his head.

"No way. That was old stuff, letting the weather

have you. We've got some class now." Wayne opened the duffel bag and pulled out a cylindrical waterproof bag that contained a three-man tent.

"Bought it last year at a rummage sale," he said. "Just in case I decided to go trucking. We sleep in the open but if it rains we can move inside."

The tent was comprised of slip-together fiberglass rods that curved to make an igloolike shelter and was up in minutes.

"And a fire," Wayne said. "We need a fire in that pit. You handle that," he added, pointing to Terry.

Terry looked for scraps of wood and didn't find any until he located a rack left by the chamber of commerce loaded with cut firewood pieces already split and dried for campers. He carried some over to the concrete pit with an iron grate on top and dropped them. "I don't have any matches."

"Later," Wayne said, positioning the tent well away from the fire. "First shelter, then food."

Waylon had set up his stove and was working at a meal by the time Terry returned with more wood, and it seemed in moments they had a camp set up, food cooking—this time a vegetable stew with ingredients from Waylon's surprise pack and Wayne's duffel bag. Wayne found matches and made a fire and they sat around it, waiting for the stew to cook, drinking hot chocolate Waylon had picked up at a truck stop along with three cups and two bottles of water.

"Oh, man, this brings back memories, doesn't it?" Wayne leaned back on an elbow and sipped the chocolate.

"Did you guys go tripping a lot?" Terry asked.

Waylon laughed. "That's the wrong term. *Trucking*, we went trucking. *Tripping* was using drugs."

Wayne nodded. "We did that, too, man. We tripped on all kinds of shi—drugs. After we came back, I don't think I was straight for two, three years."

"Back from where?"

"The 'Nam. We were in Vietnam."

Both men became quiet, looking at the fire, and Waylon spoke quietly. "Yeah, we pulled tours in the 'Nam. . . ."

"That's where we started tripping. They had drugs there that would scour your mind, man. Make you think you were inside out." Wayne sighed, remembering.

"All bad," Waylon added. "All that crap . . . Even when it was cool to do it, drugs sucked. Even when *we* did it, it was the stupid thing to do. There were garbage heads running around turning kids on—that writer and his Acid Trip bus, Timothy Leary—and everybody thought it was cool, but it wasn't. It kills everything, did then and does now. Just crap."

A mosquito fought the smoke and landed on Terry's neck and he brushed it away. "Did you guys go to Vietnam together and then just stay together afterward?"

"We worked with each other over in-country," Wayne said. "But not afterward. I bought Baby when I came home and hit the road and didn't see Waylon for four, five months. Or was it more?"

"Six," Waylon said. "Almost seven."

"Then we went trucking together."

"On bikes?"

"Just Baby. The two of us."

Terry looked at the flames for a time, thinking of what they'd said: the war, the bike, drugs—it all swirled together. Then he remembered Waylon hitting the two men in the gas station. "Is that where you learned to do that?" he asked. "You know, those two guys you hit. Did you learn that in Vietnam?"

Neither man said anything and Terry realized he'd asked something he shouldn't have and took a sip of his chocolate, which was getting cold. "I didn't mean to say anything wrong—I just didn't know."

Waylon looked up sharply. "You know who Robert E. Lee was?"

Terry nodded, glad to at last know something. "He fought for the South in the Civil War."

"Right. He commanded the South. You know what he said? He said, 'It is well war is so terrible, we should get too fond of it.' "

"What does that mean?"

"It means," Wayne cut in, standing up, "that it's time to eat."

And that was the end of conversation for the night. When they'd finished eating, they rolled out foam pads near the tent, let the fire die down, and each slid inside his bag.

Terry was using his windbreaker for a pillow and couldn't get it quite right and kept moving it around to find the most comfortable position. At last he folded and refolded it and then lay looking at the red coals of the fire. Waylon and Wayne were breathing evenly and he thought they were asleep. At last he felt his eyes closing, the warmth of the coals making him drowsy, when Waylon spoke softly.

"You're starting to learn."

"What?"

"You're starting to want to know things. More things. You asked questions, pushed. That's good— that's how you learn."

Then he was silent, his breathing smoothed, and Terry closed his eyes and let sleep come.

15

SAMUEL WAS SO OLD Terry thought he was dead when they first met.

He had awakened to the smell of Waylon making coffee and the sound of Wayne coughing softly.

They had a small breakfast of leftover stew and a doughnut each, then fired their engines and started driving. The camper was still there and Terry thought they must have been awakened by the Harley's motor, which rumbled like thunder in the morning mist, but there was no sign of life.

He still had no idea of where they were going and followed Wayne and Baby while they stopped at a grocery store and Waylon went in to buy provisions. Then they drove on, Terry expecting to drive all day, but at midmorning Wayne suddenly slowed and took a gravel side road.

It was rough and the Cat bounced enough to cause the hood to make a rattling sound where it hit the body, and Terry slowed to a virtual crawl, let Wayne get out well ahead, and just followed the dust plume from the back wheel of the Harley.

The gravel went for nearly seven miles, then turned into a two-rut road that kept Wayne active on the bike and twice snatched the wheel out of Terry's hand when the front tires caught the ruts.

"If it rains we aren't getting out of here," he said, looking at the dirt tracks. "This will turn to mud."

Waylon nodded but said nothing.

They were by this time well out into the South Dakota prairie. Terry could see for miles and there didn't seem to be anything worth going to—just grass and softly rolling hills.

But they rounded a curve and in the distance he saw what looked like a dump with an old trailer house sitting in front of it.

"Is that where we're going?" he asked Waylon.

Waylon nodded. "Samuel."

They hit a bump and Terry was thrown up and forward so hard he thought if he hadn't been belted in he would have been flipped out of the car. "I hope he's worth all this."

Wayne turned Baby into a track leading up to the trailer and Terry nosed the Cat in after him, bouncing to a stop in front of the trailer.

Close up, the place looked even worse. There was

junk and garbage everywhere—old beer bottles, food containers, trash. And the trailer was well past its prime, covered with peeling tar paper that had once been painted silver but had turned to gray.

In front of the trailer, to the side of the door, was an old recliner chair, weather-beaten with stuffing coming out of it, and sitting in the chair was a man so old he didn't look alive.

"Samuel?" Terry asked, getting out of the Cat and stretching.

Waylon nodded. "The very man."

Terry studied the old man. There was no hair left, and the face was a mass of interlocking small wrinkles, impossibly close together and so thick they almost made a texture.

Samuel gave no indication that he had seen them arrive but sat, looking out across the prairie, while Wayne went up to him.

"Hello, old friend. How are you?"

Samuel's head turned slightly and very, very slowly, and his eyes—small and dark brown but bright—peered up at Wayne.

"Who is that?" Samuel asked. The voice was as old as the body, cracked and strained and seemed to be on the edge of a hiss.

"Wayne—and Waylon. And a friend."

"It's good to have friends."

"Yes, it is."

"Did you bring sugar?"

"Yes, we did."

"It's good to have friends, but it's better to have friends with sugar."

Wayne stepped into the trailer as if he'd been there all his life, and Terry heard pots rattling and followed him in. He was still starved—couldn't seem to get enough food—and thought Wayne might be cooking.

The inside of the trailer looked like the outside. There were bits of junk everywhere, an old bunk at the end, and dozens and dozens of pictures of girls from magazines. They were taped on the walls, the ceiling, lying on the crusted table—everywhere.

Terry stopped inside the door, looking. "What . . ."

Wayne was at the stove, knocking some residue from a pan, then moved to the dish-filled sink to get water to heat in the pan. "Yeah—cool, isn't it? I could use this place for research to paint tanks. Man, some of these pictures go back a ways. Look, here's Miss August 1963—dig the hair. She'd be fifty years old or better now." He laughed. "Like me."

A million questions seemed to come at Terry but he held them, not knowing exactly where to start. Wayne put the water on the stove and then rummaged through a cupboard until he found instant coffee and a cup. He blew the cup clean, or cleaner than it was, and poured hot water and then a small spoon of coffee crystals in it. "Samuel, he likes his sugar." He turned to the screen door and yelled, "Waylon—bring the sugar."

Waylon brought a five-pound sack of sugar in, and Wayne put six heaping spoonfuls in the coffee, stirred it once, and took it out to Samuel.

Terry followed and watched the old man take the cup and drink the thick syrup down in one long draught.

Terry almost threw up, watching, but the old man smacked his lips and held the cup up to Wa~ "More."

Wayne disappeared back into the trailer. This time Terry stayed outside. Waylon kneeled on the ground in front of Samuel and waited, resting on his haunches, and Terry did the same. The sun baked the back of his neck and he felt the heat go throughout his body.

Samuel said nothing but sat breathing loudly, eyes half closed, staring out at the prairie once more.

Terry caught Waylon's eyes with his own and raised them in question, but Waylon gave an abrupt shake of his head and ended it.

Wayne came back outside with another cup and Samuel drained it as he had the first, in one long swallow, some of the fluid dribbling down his chin onto his flannel shirt. This time he did not hand the cup back but set it on the ground next to the recliner and leaned back with his eyes closed.

Terry thought he had gone to sleep, but in a moment he heard a keening sound, almost a song, very soft, almost delicate, and realized it was coming from Samuel.

Terry held his breath, listening. They were words but so faint they were nearly not there, a tiny sound.

A song?

He saw that Waylon and Wayne were smiling. So this was what they wanted? This song sound? This was what the big mystery was all about?

". . . came a row of pale riders . . ."

Terry caught some words, part of a phrase, almost music.

". . . borne in the light . . .

. . . a row of pale riders . . .

. . . passing through the night . . ."

It made no sense to Terry and he wondered if it was

supposed to, was thinking he would try to get Waylon's attention again and take him aside and ask him if he was missing everything, when Samuel's voice changed.

Low, husky, it seemed to grow younger. Samuel was still old, still bent in the chair, his eyes still closed and his head thrown back, but the voice, the voice grew in strength, intensity, depth, volume.

It startled Terry and he nearly jumped back.

". . . they came *right* here, past here, all of them, one upon the other upon the other through here out there where the sun goes, horses dead and dying. . . ."

His voice trailed off, ended.

Terry couldn't stand it. "Who? Who came through here?"

Waylon snapped him a look—Terry couldn't tell if it was in anger or surprise—but it didn't matter.

"All the Sioux," Samuel said. "The People—they came through here and passed on horses dead and dying one step ahead of the soldiers, running, running from the blue men on gray horses, through here while the farmers shot at them. . . ."

Again he trailed off, seemed to doze.

"When did this happen?" Terry asked again.

"During the big war."

"He means the Civil War," Waylon said. "The Sioux rose up in 1861 and the army went after them."

". . . caught them, caught them and put them in chains and boxes and took them back to hang; three hundred of them to hang. . . ." Samuel took several breaths. "Three hundred to jerk on ropes, swing in the Minnesota sun. . . ."

This time he stopped, or seemed to, and Waylon

finished it. "They wanted to hang three hundred. Lincoln stepped in and commuted sentences to let them off. But they still hung thirty-seven. All at once."

"Here?"

Waylon shook his head. "No, back in Minnesota. But they came through here. This is where the army came for them, caught them, took them back."

"And he *saw* them? A hundred and thirty years ago?"

Waylon shook his head. "No. But he remembers."

Terry stared at Samuel, then back at Waylon. "But that was before he was born—how can he remember?"

Wayne stood. He'd been squatting near the trailer, listening. "He just does. . . ."

". . . things don't die," Samuel said, his voice soft again, singsongy. "They just change. The earth that was here then is still here, the rocks are still here, the dirt, the sky, the sun—it is still here, all here. So, then, are they—the ones on dead and dying ponies. Their cries are still here, it is just a matter of listening for them, hearing them. . . ."

And he grew silent.

This time Terry did not question him but sat, looking as Samuel had looked, out across the prairie, trying to see it, hear it, but he could not.

Samuel's breathing grew even and Waylon stood and whispered, "He's sleeping." He moved away from Samuel and up to the trailer, motioning for Terry and Wayne to follow him.

"Let's clean the place up," Waylon said. "And cook some food for him. It doesn't look like he's eaten in a long time."

So while Samuel slept they cleaned the trailer—

Terry thought it should have been hosed out—washed dishes, mopped the floors, and wiped everything down, working around the pictures.

When they finished, Terry thought it still looked pretty rough but was glad to stop. Waylon had found cans of spaghetti and was heating up a big pot of it, mixing in some stewed tomatoes he'd brought from the store, and he left it simmering while they went outside to take a break.

Samuel was still sleeping soundly; the afternoon sun coming back over the trailer put him in the cool shade of the wall, and the three of them went out away from the trailer and sat in the grass, relaxing.

Waylon had also made coffee—he seemed to live on coffee—and he and Wayne sipped it while they sat. Terry poked at the dirt with a stick.

"I don't get it," he finally said.

"Which part don't you get?" Waylon asked.

"Well, any of it. I don't know why we're here, why we're talking to this crazy old man. . . ."

"He's not crazy," Waylon said, his voice sharpening. "Not even a little bit."

"But he talks about things like they just happened, and he couldn't know all that, all that he talks about."

"He does know it though." Wayne shrugged. "I was like you when I came—didn't believe. But he's right. He sees things, knows things, hears things. And if you listen to him you can learn."

"Is that why we're here—to listen to him?"

"Exactly." Waylon nodded. "That's it exactly. He's like . . . like a living book. He'll tell you stuff that hasn't been written, will never be written, but you can learn from it. We came here back in seventy-three—twenty years ago. Came from the 'Nam. Came from all that. Mean and hard and looking for something, some way to live. They told us about him then, and we came."

"Who told you?" Terry looked across to Samuel, who was not moving, seemed impossibly small in the recliner.

"People. People who trucked and came here and learned from him. That's why we brought you—brought ourselves back."

"How did you know he was still alive?"

"We didn't. But if he'd died we would have heard. Somebody would have said."

"Here we are." Terry sighed. "I haven't the slightest idea *where* we are, but here we are. . . ."

"It's like this," Wayne said. "Be honest. Do you know more now than when we came—know more about America?"

Terry thought about what he'd learned, what Samuel had said. "Well, yes. I do. About the Sioux thing."

"And do you want to know more?"

He thought again and realized that he did—that he was immensely curious. "Yes."

"There it is, man." Wayne turned to Waylon. "I mean there it is—just like before. It still works. Samuel still works."

Waylon smiled and nodded. "It's a start."

16

"How old is he?"

It was evening and Samuel was still sleeping in the chair. Waylon had found a blanket in the trailer and covered the old man, tucking him in carefully. Then the three of them had made a fire pit and located their bed-rolls near it, made a fire, helped Wayne put up the tent—although it didn't look at all like rain; the sky was clear and the stars seemed so close they could be touched.

They had eaten spaghetti and were lying around the fire, propped on elbows, and Terry was looking to the recliner where Samuel hadn't moved.

"Nobody knows. He was old when we came here before—twenty years ago. A hundred, a hundred and ten, twenty. He's past counting." Waylon took a long pull of his coffee. "Past aging. He'll just be that way now until . . . well, until he's gone."

Terry stared at Samuel. It was dark, but in the light from the fire the recliner and the man looked yellow. "He looks . . . gone . . . now."

Wayne nodded. "Right. But he's not. He'll come up and start talking again. You want to be listening when it comes."

"Has he been here all the time?"

"Yeah. Some say he's an Indian, but I heard he punched cows for a while back when. Nobody is sure how he started, just how he is now. Back in the sixties, seventies, must have been hundreds, maybe thousands of people came past, talking to him, listening to him."

Samuel coughed and the three became silent, listening, but he didn't say anything further. Waylon used the silence to lay back and Terry did the same.

He pulled his bag up around his shoulders to keep the cool air out, positioned his windbreaker under his head, and lay looking up. Out of the corner of his eye he saw the Cat and Baby sitting near each other, the starlight gleaming on the chrome, and he tried to remember his other life, how much time had passed. It simply didn't come. He remembered his parents, that he had parents, but how they looked was fuzzy—he could remember his house, his room better—and he realized with a start that it had only been six, seven days since he'd gone. Since he'd met Waylon in the rain.

And here he was. On the prairie, listening to an old man, camped with a couple of holdovers from the sixties, learning about a world he didn't know existed.

Life . . . , he thought. *Life rolls funny if you don't watch it.*

He closed his eyes and was asleep before he thought another word.

". . . voted for the son of a bitch and he let us down. . . ."

Terry wasn't sure how long he had slept but it was still dark when the voice brought him up. He opened his eyes and rolled over. The fire was well out, the ashes cold, and the sound was coming from Samuel.

Terry unzipped the bag and wrapped it around his shoulders and stood—saw that Waylon was up and doing the same, though Wayne was still asleep—and moved to Samuel's side, where they sat against the trailer, bundled in their bags.

"Who?" Terry asked, but Waylon held a hand on his shoulder and pressed him into quiet.

"You don't have to ask," Waylon whispered. "Just let him talk."

". . . there were dreams everywhere, so many dreams you couldn't count them, and Hoover got in and they *all* went to hell. . . ."

He took a breath. Terry thought it must be three or four in the morning. He didn't have a watch. He had one flash of thought: *I'm sitting in the middle of the night listening to this. . . .* But it trailed off and Samuel started again.

". . . people died. Jumped from buildings and died because of money. Farms died. People went for food, wanted for food, and starved. And then the droughts came, droughts and dust, dust in your lungs, dust in the cracks of your eyes, dust for air, dust for food, dust for death . . ."

He stopped again and Waylon leaned over to whisper, "The depression. He's talking about the depression."

"What?"

"A bad time. Back in the thirties. When corrupt politicians bled the country dry and a big drought came. Same as the eighties and Reagan . . ."

". . . women marrying in dust, living in dust, loving in dust, burying their babies in dust . . . the sky gone in dust . . . the sun gone in dust . . ."

And Samuel stopped again, breathing deeply.

Waylon sat silently, thinking, and Terry looked out at the dark sky, trying to see the horizon, and tried to envision what it must have been like sixty years earlier. Once a teacher had talked of the depression but he had just said there were long lines at soup kitchens and something called the dust bowl. Somehow it didn't seem like it happened to people.

Until now.

Now it seemed real. Something in the way Samuel talked, the way his voice worked, made it seem real— the dust, the people, the babies crying. All real.

"He's asleep again," Waylon said. "I'm not sure for how long. We'll just stay next to him and wait until he wakes up."

They sat the rest of the night, leaning against the trailer next to the recliner, sleeping, and that's the way Wayne found them in the morning, still dozing with Samuel sound asleep between them and, indeed, Samuel did not awaken until nearly noon.

17

THEY STAYED all that day and night and left the following morning. They cooked for him and made more coffee, thick with sugar, and sat by the fire when he slept and next to him when he spoke.

Samuel talked four more times at length: about draft riots in New York during the Civil War, about an influenza epidemic in St. Louis at the turn of the century that killed forty percent of the people there, a short bit about one of his wives—he'd had several but nobody was sure how many—and how good she cooked, and a story about two women who took a wagon across during the Oregon Trail days.

Then he stopped and stared at Waylon and said, "It's good you came. Next time bring sugar again. It's good to have friends with sugar."

Waylon nodded. "It was good to see you again."

And they packed their bedrolls on the bike and the car and drove away, Terry watching in the rearview mirror until Samuel, the trailer, the junk were all out of sight.

They were well off the gravel, back on the main road before Terry spoke.

"Will he be, you know, all right?"

Waylon smiled. "He's tougher than he looks. When people take care of him he soaks it up, but when he's alone he gets along all right. And I think somebody from the county comes out and checks on him now and then."

"And all that stuff that he says, that's all true?"

"I don't know about all of it. But the things I checked on, or know myself, are dead right. There were draft riots and a Sioux uprising and a dust bowl and a flu epidemic in St. Louis—all those things happened. I don't know about his wives or the two women who took a wagon to Oregon, but I'd bet it's right."

They came out to the highway then and Wayne, who had been riding Baby ahead of them, dropped back alongside and signaled them to stop.

"Whose turn?"

"What?" Terry thought Wayne was talking to him, but when he looked he saw that Wayne was looking across, smiling at Waylon.

"I guess mine," Waylon said. "Then Terry's."

"What are you guys talking about?"

Wayne laughed. "Trucking—you take turns deciding where to go, when. All of it. So I was the one who decided to visit Samuel. It's somebody else's turn now."

"Mine," Waylon said. "Unless you want it."

Terry shook his head. "No. I don't know for sure what I'm doing yet."

Wayne laughed, cracking the throttle on Baby, letting the pipes burble. "That's it, man. None of us know what we're doing. Never have, never will. It don't mean nothing."

Terry looked to Waylon. "So—what do we do?"

Waylon thought a minute, then smiled up at Wayne. "We're in South Dakota, right?"

Wayne nodded.

"Then it has to be Deadwood." Waylon shrugged. "If it's South Dakota, it has to be Deadwood. That's where the action is."

"West it is," Wayne said, kicking Baby into gear and heading onto the road.

Terry shifted—he drove the Cat automatically now, completely without thinking. It had become an extension of him, the steering, the sound of the motor, the feel of the tires on the road—all of it a part of him—and he wondered if Wayne had been right. If he was a natural. Maybe he ought to think about that, about doing something with cars. Motors.

It was still early in the morning and as Wayne found a highway going west, Terry followed, matching the bike's speed—just at sixty. He glanced at Waylon out of the corner of his eye, wanted to ask him how far it was to Deadwood, but Waylon was reading, hunkered down with a paperback volume of Shakespeare, frowning while he read, and Terry didn't want to interrupt him.

There was an atlas behind the seat or in the side pocket, he couldn't remember which, and he could look it up himself. But he decided against it. The morning sun was on the back of his neck, the car running smoothly, the tires hissing on the asphalt—what did it matter how far it was, or if they ever got there at all? What was Deadwood, anyway?

Just a place, he thought. *Another place.*

A meadowlark sang next to the car as it passed and as soon as one did, it seemed dozens of them cut loose. Fence post after fence post had a meadowlark sitting on it, or so it appeared, and as the Cat passed them they all sang.

"It's like a chorus, isn't it?"

Terry jumped at the voice and turned to see Waylon looking at him.

"The meadowlarks," Waylon said. "Pretty, aren't they?"

Terry nodded and Waylon went back to his book, but the silence had been broken.

"You read that a lot, don't you?"

Waylon looked up again. "Shakespeare? Yeah—all the time."

"How come?"

"Because he's absolutely, without any doubt, completely and far away the best writer of the English language who ever lived."

"Really?"

"Totally. If you want to learn, you study winners— you study the best. And I want to learn."

"You do?" Terry veered slightly around a crack in the road, following Wayne's move ahead of him. "That's hard to believe."

"Why?"

"I thought, I mean I sort of figured you and Wayne kind of knew it all."

Waylon snorted, then laughed. "Know it all—hell, we don't know *anything*. We're still trying to figure out the basics—you know, like what we ought to be when we grow up."

"But you're . . ."

"Old. Yeah, I know. But that's what I mean. We don't have a clue. I know a guy, lives out in Los Angeles, my age plus a little, maybe forty-six, -seven, just decided he wants to be a doctor. So he's going to school, studying, taking all the courses—thing is, by the time he's done he'll be too old to start practicing."

"Then why do it?"

"Because that's what he wants to be. He finally worked it out." Waylon laughed. "I haven't even gotten that far. 'Know it all. . . .' Oh, man, that's good. Wayne will love that."

He opened the Shakespeare book again and started to read, and Terry went back to driving, wondering if he should decide on what to be when he grew up now so he wouldn't still be thinking of it in thirty, forty years.

Deadwood, Terry found, was on the western end of South Dakota. They had started on the eastern end of South Dakota so they had to drive end to end across the state—which would normally take between six and seven hours, or a bit less if they held the speed up.

That would be normal driving on the highway.

But Waylon signaled Wayne over to the side and insisted that they take back roads, side highways, county roads.

"You'll see more," he said, as Terry followed Wayne through small towns and farms that gave way to ranches.

It became flat, totally, unbelievably flat and treeless. At first Terry didn't like it. But soon he found himself drawn to the horizon, pulled into going ahead, seeing ahead, being ahead, and he started liking the huge sky, the wide open feel of the country.

Once when they stopped for gas he looked at the atlas and saw a park marked Badlands.

"What does that mean, 'Badlands'?" he asked Waylon.

"Rough country—like it says, bad land."

"Worse than this?" Terry waved at the prairie around the gas station.

Waylon smiled. "Nothing there, nothing growing. Nothing but dinosaur bones."

"Can we go see it?"

"That," Waylon said, hanging the hose back in the cradle, "is what trucking is all about."

And even with that, even with stopping at the Badlands they would have made Deadwood that evening, and Terry had come to count on it, was looking forward to it.

Except that Waylon saw a sign on a side road that pointed to a religious commune.

"Don't you wonder," he asked, "how they live?"

And because he didn't know yet, didn't understand yet what Waylon meant—not *Don't you wonder how they live* but *Let's go* see *how they live*—because he hadn't come to know Waylon and Wayne as well as he would, Terry said:

"Yeah . . ."

18

"WE CAN'T GO IN THERE."

Terry stopped the Cat at the entrance to the commune. Wayne stopped in back of them, following after
Terry flashed his lights and brought him back. They had
moved down a gravel road for three miles, following
signs with a cross and a flower on them, and were now
at a driveway leading under a metal arch with a steel
cross welded in the middle. It was all painted white and
seemed well kept. The driveway itself went into a stand
of trees and a huge white house could be seen over them.

"It says Welcome to All Who Believe," Waylon said,
noting a sign to the side of the entry. "Don't you
believe?"

"Well, I guess so. But . . ."

"Then we go in. We're here to learn. Let's go see what they do in a religious commune."

Terry put the Cat in gear and nosed in the driveway, heard the Harley rumbling in back of him, and kept it low, moving slowly all the way up to the house.

Everything about the place seemed to be white and well tended and very prosperous. The house was more like an old-fashioned hotel, a large box with a peaked roof and what seemed to be dozens and dozens of small windows.

Out of sight from the road but coming into view as they drove into the yard, there were large, metal open-front buildings with tractors, combines, and other machinery inside. It all seemed new.

There were children running in the yard, playing, and they stopped and stared at the Cat and the Harley as Terry, Waylon, and Wayne drove up. The children were six or seven—there were eight of them—and they were all boys wearing dark pants and white shirts and felt hats that made them look like they were mimicking grown-ups.

Initially no adults showed, but as Waylon got out of the Cat two men came walking up from one of the machine sheds. They were wearing white shirts, felt hats, and black pants and suspenders—larger versions of the boys—and they walked slowly, looking at the car and the Harley and particularly at Wayne, who looked every inch the biker.

"This is nuts," Terry said. "I'm really feeling embarrassed. . . ."

"It gets better," Waylon said, looking over the top

of the car at the men, who were getting close. "Good morning! Isn't it a beautiful day?"

The men stopped, half smiling. One nodded and the other stood silently, staring openly at the Harley.

"We were driving by and saw your sign and my . . . nephew here wanted to know more about you. Is it all right if we talk to you for a bit?"

Terry wished he could curl up in the car and hide, wondered what would happen if he just backed up and drove away.

"What would you like to know?" the man who had nodded asked.

"Well, I'm not sure." Waylon turned to Terry. "What was it you wanted to know?"

"Me?"

"Well, you're the one who wanted to come and talk to them."

"I wasn't . . . sure. I wasn't sure what I wanted to know." Terry recovered quickly. "Just how it is here, how it is to live here."

The man nodded. "We get people who are curious all the time. If you wait here I will go and return with Peter."

They talked funny, Terry decided, or different. Shaping each word carefully to say it right or something.

The young man who had spoken went off, but the other one was still studying the Harley. Finally he coughed softly and smiled at Wayne.

"That is a beautiful motor cycle." He said it slowly, the words *motor* and *cycle* separated and spoken distinctly.

"It's Baby," Wayne said.

"Baby?"

"The name of the bike—motorcycle. I call her Baby."

"You have named the motor cycle?"

"Right on. She's my friend."

"But it is a machine, yes?"

Wayne seemed shocked. "Machine? Baby? This is a bike, this is a Harley, a *Harley*, man—it's a ride, you know what I mean? It's not a machine. It's like . . . like a way to live."

The young man nodded slowly, as if understanding, but his expression was clearly bewildered and he seemed about to say more when the first man came out of the house.

He was being led by an older man—Terry thought in his sixties or seventies, older than Wayne and Waylon—who came forward, smiling, and held his hand out to Waylon.

"Good day. I am Peter. Can I help you to know something?"

Waylon shook hands. "My nephew here was curious as to how you lived here, and I said I would bring him in to ask. If you don't mind?"

"Not at all. Not at all." Peter turned to Terry. "What is it you would like to know?"

He had smiling eyes and gray hair, long enough to just cover the tops of his ears, and gray eyebrows and nostril and ear hair that stuck out.

"I'm not sure." Terry shot a look at Waylon. "Just what it's like to live here, I guess."

"We work together and live in God's way," Peter said. "It is very simple to do. Would you like to look around?"

Terry, still sitting in the car, nodded and realized with the nod that he truly did. He opened the door and climbed out, stretched, and was surprised to find Peter holding his hand out. Terry shook hands awkwardly and realized it was the first time in his life he'd ever done it, shaken hands with somebody.

"After I show you how we live it will be time for the midday meal. Would you please join us for food?"

Waylon said nothing and Terry was going to turn him down—it seemed a bother—but Wayne smiled.

"Far out. We'd love it, man."

Peter led off with the three of them following, and Terry looked back to find one of the other young men following them as well as all the boys who had been playing in the yard. The man who had been talking with Wayne about the bike hung back and stood next to Baby, staring intently, as if to memorize every bolt and bit of chrome.

Peter saw it as well and stopped. "Joseph. We are going now."

Joseph looked up. "It is so shiny."

"Yes. It is. But it is a graven image. You must come now."

"Yes, Papa."

And Joseph came with them, though looking back once at Baby.

"I must ask you not to take photographs," Peter said. "It is against our practices to keep images."

Waylon nodded. "We don't have a camera."

"That is fine."

He led them to the machine barns where there were new tractors, other equipment looking clean and well cared for, and other young men working, all dressed the same.

"You use modern equipment," Waylon said. "Not horses and buggies?"

Peter nodded. "That is correct. We are not as fundamental as other sects—at least not in our working methods. But in our beliefs, yes. We believe the same, we just work the land differently."

Peter took them to a shed where a machine run by a middle-aged man was making brooms. "For selling in the stores," Peter said, "to make money to buy what material goods we need."

After the broom shed he took them to the beehives, where a man was inspecting combs to see that the bees were making honey, and to hog pens and a pasture full of sleek black-and-white cows.

"It all looks so . . ." Terry thought for the words. ". . . fat. Everything looks full and fat somehow."

Peter smiled. "It is so that our work brings forth much fruit."

It all fascinated Terry and he pointed at things and asked questions, and they walked around the farm for half an hour and more while Peter showed them their lives, and they were moving back toward the house when it struck Terry that Waylon and Wayne had both grown silent, seemed to be thinking, but he had seen them do it before and thought it must be some memory bothering them.

Waylon rubbed the back of his neck and looked around the farm. "Where are the women?"

Peter hadn't heard the question and turned. "What did you say?"

"It's all boys and men. I haven't seen any girls or women," Waylon said. "Where are they?"

"They are inside," Peter said. "It is not fit for them to meet strangers. They are inside preparing the meal. Come, let us eat."

He led them to the big house, passing through a side door that led to an entrance hallway with coats and boots hung on pegs on the wall. To the left of the hall there was a doorway leading into a kitchen that Peter showed them in passing.

It was huge—like a kitchen for a large school—and as Peter had said the women were there.

They were each dressed in a long-sleeved, long, dark dress and wore their hair up with a small white cap covering it, and not one of them looked at Wayne or Waylon or Terry. There were little girls and teenage girls and young women and older women, all working over the stoves and pots that bubbled and hissed.

The kitchen was viciously hot—no air-conditioning—and the dresses looked uncomfortable. Many of the women and girls were covered with perspiration, their dresses sticking to them, but they seemed cheerful for all that.

Peter led the men out of the kitchen and to the dining hall, a large room with windows on the east side of the house, which was filling up with men and boys, all sitting at long tables where there were plates and silverware waiting.

Peter directed them to a table. "Please sit. They will bring food soon."

The three of them sat, Waylon and Terry on one side, Wayne on the other with Peter at the end.

No sooner had they settled in than the women started bringing pots of food in from the kitchen on carts, ladling steaming potatoes and meat onto the plates.

It smelled delicious and Terry picked up his fork to mash the potatoes—keenly aware that he hadn't had a proper meal in over three weeks—but noticed that nobody else was eating and put the fork down.

Peter waited until the room was silent. "We give thanks now to the Lord who gives us all, shows us all, is all. Amen."

The rest of the room—there were at least thirty boys and men—chorused *Amen* and then fell to eating.

There was no talk. *They eat fast, swallowing hugely, like wolves,* Terry thought, and he found himself doing the same.

It tasted as good as it smelled, and he ate until he couldn't move, couldn't get another bite down, whereupon the girls and women came back with pies—a whole cart of steaming cherry and peach pies. Terry had thought he was full but the smell of the pies started the hunger again, and he ate a huge slab of cherry pie and was finished with it when he saw that Waylon had not taken any pie and had eaten only a bite or two of his meat and potatoes.

Wayne had eaten, but only a little and the rest was uneaten.

There was the look again between Wayne and Waylon—the quiet, still look Terry had seen before—

and Wayne set his fork down softly next to the plate and nodded and that was it.

"What's the matter with you guys?" Terry swallowed the last of the pie. "Why aren't you eating?"

Waylon said nothing, but Peter had heard Terry and he looked up over a huge forkful of pie.

"Yes. Why is it that you do not eat?"

Wayne looked at Waylon.

Waylon studied Peter, his eyes cool, expression flat. "Why aren't the girls and women eating?"

Something in Waylon's voice caught Peter. He put his fork down, sat up straighter. "They do not eat with the men."

"Why?"

"It is forbidden. They eat in the kitchen."

"Why?"

"Because it is so. It is in the Bible."

"That women don't eat with men?"

"Yes."

"No," Waylon said, his voice moving now to an edge. "It isn't."

"Waylon . . . ," Wayne cut in. "Maybe we ought to go."

"Well, it doesn't," Waylon said. "I've read the Bible, studied it. It doesn't say anywhere in there that men and women can't eat together. That's some crap these bas—"

"Waylon. We have to leave, now."

Waylon stood—his shoulders loose, his hands hanging at his sides—and Terry thought, *Anything can happen now, here. Anything.* They were in a room full of young and old men, twenty, thirty of them. Strong men.

The room grew quiet. Men put their eating utensils down, watched Waylon.

"Yes," Peter said. "I think it is time that you should go now."

"I will when the girls eat," Waylon said. "In here."

"We do not live that way."

"You're going to wish like hell you did," Waylon said. "In about one minute."

Wayne moved around the table. "Come on, Waylon. This isn't the right place to do this."

"It never is."

Waylon stood for fifteen, twenty seconds. Terry stared at him. Then Wayne touched Waylon's shoulder, pushed it, pulled it a small amount, and something seemed to go out of Waylon, like a spring unwinding slowly, and it was over.

"We'll leave now," Wayne said softly. "Thank you for the food."

He moved Waylon easily toward the door, the whole mess hall watching, Terry following. Just as they were at the door, Peter said softly, "I am sorry for you."

Waylon stopped, his back stiffened, but Wayne nudged him and he went through the door and out of the building to the waiting Cat.

Terry fired the engine, wrapped it up twice to get the noise, heard Wayne do the same with Baby, and they left.

Waylon said nothing, sat in silence for a good ten miles, all the way back onto the highway, and remained quiet until Terry leaned over.

"You all right?"

Waylon jumped, startled. "What?"

"You all right?"

"Sure. Why shouldn't I be all right?"

"It was just all that, back at the commune. You seemed really upset."

"It's slavery. They keep those women and girls like slaves, servants. Weren't you upset?"

Terry thought a minute. "Well, no. I didn't think of it."

"Next time"—Waylon looked at him, the wind ruffling the hair around his bald spot, watched Terry for a long time, until Terry was uncomfortable—"think of it."

"I will," Terry said. "I mean, I'll try."

"Good. Now let's go see Deadwood."

19

IT STARTED TO RAIN as they came to the outskirts of Deadwood. They had run all day from the commune in good weather but after dark, clouds started to form in small clumps, and by ten o'clock there was lightning hitting trees along the road, and it started to sprinkle as they drove through the pine forests approaching Deadwood.

Outside of the town proper—which Terry found to be small and busy—Waylon pointed to a small motel sign that said Piney Wood Inn. Phones.

"There. Pull in there."

"A motel?"

"Yes. It's going to pour like hell and we don't want to camp."

"But won't it cost a lot of money?"

"I'll pay."

"I didn't mean that. I have some money, too. I just meant that, well, you know, isn't part of trucking to not spend much money?" Terry pulled into the motel and stopped in front of a small door next to a sign that said Office.

Waylon laughed. "That's how it seemed—none of us had any. Except for Wayne."

"Wayne had money?"

"His repair check. Got it every month. Still does."

"Repair check?"

"They blew him up a little," Waylon said. "In Vietnam. Parts of him don't work."

Terry watched Wayne pull the Harley up and reach back for a poncho, which he had already removed from his duffel bag. He looked so healthy, so tough.

"What parts?"

"That," Waylon said, climbing out of the car, "is something you don't ask."

"Oh."

"Cover the cab—it's going to fill." Waylon disappeared into the motel office and Terry scrambled to get the plastic tarp over the cab just as it started to pour. He crouched beneath the tarp and peeked out to see Wayne standing at the side of Baby, holding his poncho out to cover the bike seat as he would hold it to protect a friend.

Waylon came out in a minute, dangling a key. "Room twenty-six. Follow me."

He walked down the row of small bungalows until he came to the right one, and Terry and Wayne followed with the car and bike. At twenty-six, Waylon opened the door and went in. Terry pulled up and jumped out, covered the cab with the tarp and pulled it into place with bungee cords, and ran for the door just as Wayne got there without his poncho on. He had used it to cover Baby.

The rain roared down by this time and they left the door open to watch it for a time. It was eleven o'clock and Terry was exhausted and thinking of how they would sleep. There was only one bed in the room.

"We'll draw straws for it," Waylon said, noting Terry's interest. "Losers sleep on the floor. When we get back."

"Back? Where are we going?"

"To show you Deadwood."

"It's nearly midnight."

"Exactly." Wayne laughed. "Exactly. Like Deadwood doesn't come alive until midnight, and then it never sleeps."

We may go, Terry thought, *but I won't see anything.*

They made quick trips to the Cat and brought their gear inside. Waylon put the guitar on the bed, with the case open, and then went to the phone and dialed a number.

"Yes. Please send a cab to room twenty-six of the Piney Wood Inn." He hung up.

"A cab?"

"It's raining. We don't want to walk. Besides, we need information."

"What kind of information?"

"We have to find a game."

"Game?"

"Poker."

"That's what Deadwood is all about," Wayne added. "It's bikers in the summer and poker all the time."

"You gamble?" Terry leaned against the door.

"No." Waylon shook his head. "I play poker. There's a big difference. Poker is skill, not gambling. There are legal games here in poker parlors that we could go to, but you're too young to get in so we have to find a private game. Cab drivers know everything. . . . Ahh, and here he is."

They scooted from the bungalow door to the cab and piled in.

"Where to?" The cabbie was thin, wiry. He had a cigarette hanging out of the corner of his mouth and the inside of the cab smelled like a mixture of stale smoke and week-old vomit. Terry cracked the window.

"Looking for a hold-'em game," Waylon said.

"You came to the right place." The cabbie snorted. "Hell, that's all we got here is poker parlors—'less you're looking for the other thing."

"No. A game. But it has to be a side game. They won't let the kid in a parlor—he's too young."

The cabbie smiled. "I know just the place."

"And safe. I don't want somebody jumping us when we get there."

Terry grinned and turned to look out the window. *God help anybody,* he thought, *who jumped Waylon.*

"It's run by an old woman named Annie," the cabbie said. "She's eighty-four and keeps a little automatic in her purse in her lap. It's a *very* safe game. . . ."

"What kind of limit?"

"No limit—table stakes."

"That sounds right." Waylon nodded. "Take us away."

The cabbie drove exactly three blocks, turned right, and stopped in front of a log cabin that had seen better days. It was stuck in among some brush and other newer buildings and was so small Terry didn't see how there could be anything inside but a cot or a table. The windows were covered with plywood.

The cabbie opened the door for them and they stepped into a room so brightly lit it hurt Terry's eyes and he had to close them for a moment.

There were five men and a woman sitting at a green table in the middle of the one-room cabin. At least half the men were smoking, but the room was clear of smoke and Terry saw and heard the reason as they came in. Set off in a corner on a two-by-four stand was a huge air cleaner, whirring and hissing away.

Facing the door was Annie. She was playing but looked up and smiled when they came in the door.

"Room for two," she said.

Wayne shook his head. "I'm not a player. Too damn dumb—all I do is lose."

"So much the better."

Terry had trouble not staring at Annie. She was old, like the cabbie said, with wrinkles and gray hair, but she was still pretty in some way he couldn't understand. Her hair was long and full and braided neatly down her back and her cheekbones were high with tipped-up green eyes that looked full of humor and something else as well— something that made Terry think of girls he knew in school, pictures he had seen, movies about love.

"Is it all right for the kid to watch?" Waylon moved around the table next to Annie and took an empty chair. "I'm trying to teach him the finer things in life."

Annie nodded. "They've got to learn, don't they?"

"How about the rest of you guys?" Waylon asked.

"I said it was all right," Annie answered. "That makes it all right with everybody—don't it, boys?"

The men, a mixture of young and middle-aged, one old, almost all overweight, nodded and smiled up at Terry.

Wayne moved to a box in the corner and sat down facing the door, lowered his head, and as near as Terry could tell was instantly asleep.

"We're playing hold-'em," Annie said. "Straight Texas hold-'em, high-low split. You know the game?"

Waylon nodded. "What's the buy-in?"

"Three hundred minimum, but most are buying in for five or better."

"Give me a grand."

Waylon took a wad of hundred-dollar bills out of his pocket and Terry stared openly. He somehow had thought of Waylon as broke, or not really very rich. There were at least sixty, seventy hundred-dollar bills in the wad—six or seven thousand dollars.

Waylon peeled ten of them off and handed them to Annie, who pushed several stacks of chips over to sit in front of Waylon.

"No limit," Annie said. "Even on first bet. You can't check and raise. Other than that, straight poker. Ante is a dollar. House rakes five dollars a pot. Any questions?"

Waylon shook his head and Annie picked up the cards, shuffled them professionally, the cards flying together. She dealt each player two cards, face down, then set the deck down and took two chips out of the ante in the middle and put them on top of the deck.

"Open deck," she said. "You bet." She pointed at Waylon, who was sitting to her left.

Waylon looked at his cards without taking them off the table, cupping one hand and using the other to curl the edges up slightly to see what they were. Terry couldn't see them at all, nor could any of the others at the table.

"Pull up a box," Annie said to Terry, smiling. "And watch your daddy win."

"Uncle," Waylon said. "I'm his uncle. His father is . . . gone."

"Ahh. These things happen."

"Yes."

"And your bet?"

"Fifty dollars." Waylon pulled five ten-dollar chips off his stack and put them in the pot. Some of the men called—matched it—some threw their hands in. When it came around to the man sitting on Annie's right—a heavy-set man with a red face, smoking a cigar that one of the other men had called a dog turd—the man added ten more chips.

"Raise a hundred."

Annie threw her hand in and it came to Waylon. He stared at the pot, his eyes glazed a bit, then nodded. "I'll raise. Your hundred and four more."

Terry swallowed. Waylon hadn't been sitting at the table for six minutes and he had over five hundred dollars in the pot. And they'd only been dealt two cards each.

This heavier bet made all the men fold until it came back around to the red-faced man.

He sat, staring at the pot, his eyes glazed as Waylon's had been. A beat, two, a full thirty seconds.

Then he threw his hand in and sighed. "Take it."

Terry realized he'd been holding his breath and he took a lungful of air. Waylon raked the pot and Annie handed him the deck.

"You won it all—high and low—pot, money, everything. . . ."

"You were buying it," the red-faced man said, his eyes on the edge of hard. "Bluffing."

"You could have called it." Waylon shrugged. "Four hundred and you could have seen the cards."

"Next time."

"Fine."

Terry had no true idea of what had happened except that Waylon had bet five hundred and fifty dollars on two cards and won because nobody else would call his bet.

This time Waylon dealt, the same game, and for a change the hand played out. He dealt two cards face down to each player, the man to his left bet twenty dollars, everybody called—Waylon didn't raise—then he dealt three cards face up in the middle of the table and everybody looked at their hole cards again.

Annie sighed and threw her hand in. "Bad flop," she said. "You guys play. I'm out of this one." She turned to Terry. "You know how to play?"

He shook his head. "I know a little about poker, what the cards mean. But not this."

"This is poker. You get two cards down, then three

up, then one more up, and one more up. Everybody plays their two cards and the five cards in the middle as part of their hand. It's really straight seven-card stud except we all use those cards."

"And high-low," added a man across the table, tall, thin, wearing a down vest though the temperature had to be over ninety in the room. "The split."

"Oh. Yes. The highest and lowest hand split the pot. That makes the betting a little looser."

Terry nodded but he still didn't understand it—just snatches. He was drawn back to the pot. The first three cards face up in the middle had triggered betting and the pile of chips grew rapidly until he guessed there was close to two thousand dollars in the pot.

Waylon dealt another card face up.

Everybody bet again, except that this time when it came back around to Waylon, he stacked all his money in. "I'll raise three hundred more and I'm all in."

Other people called, added money until the pot was close to four thousand dollars.

They had to declare if they were going high or low. Everybody went high except Waylon and the man with the red face, who both went low.

Terry looked at the cards in the middle of the table.

There was an ace, a five, a three, a king, and a queen.

The high hand was won by the thin man with the down vest. The red-faced man turned his hand up.

"I have a six, four."

Waylon said nothing but turned his cards over. He was holding a deuce and a four, which gave him a lower hand than the other.

"You get half the pot," Annie said. She raked the

whole pot and started to stack the chips in two even piles, one for the high winner, the other for Waylon.

"You should have bet the hand." The red-faced man's voice was brittle.

"I did." Waylon shrugged. "All I had."

"Next time buy more chips."

Waylon said nothing, but out of the corner of his eye Terry noticed that Wayne had come awake. There was no movement. His eyes merely opened, stayed open, and didn't miss anything that went on in the room. It was like a cat watching something it was going to pounce on.

"I won't need to," Waylon said. "I just won all these." And again that quiet sound in his voice, that still menace that had happened before at the religious commune. Wayne moved behind them. Moved his shoulders.

"Three seconds," Annie said.

"What?" Waylon said to her but kept his eyes across the table, watching as Wayne watched.

"Three seconds are up. We get into these little tiffs now and then, over poker. But you're only allowed three seconds. Burk knows that, don't you, Burk?"

The red-faced man looked at Annie and then back to Waylon and slowly nodded. "Maybe later?"

"Whatever." Waylon turned to Annie. "Good rule—the three-second rule."

"I thought so. It saves trouble."

The man on Waylon's left scraped up the cards and shuffled and began to deal the next hand. Terry watched Wayne close his eyes again and apparently drop into deep sleep, and he turned back to the game.

He knew some of poker—what beat what, a pair is beat by two pair, two pair by three of a kind, what a straight was (five consecutively numbered cards) and a flush (five cards in one suit). But this game was more complicated. It wasn't just the best hand, it was the best and the lowest at the same time, so even if there wasn't a good high hand they might be betting on their low hand.

The betting was wild. Soon a hundred, two hundred became the minimum bet, and Terry saw several pots that had six or eight thousand dollars in them. Waylon didn't win them all, didn't play each hand. Often he threw his hand in with bad cards. But when he did stay in a hand, he bet heavily, always raising, and while sometimes he lost, more often he won. He played every hand with the same look on his face, staring blankly at the center of the table, his eyes seemingly glazed while he bet or waited for somebody else to bet.

But none of it—the playing, Waylon, the long day, the problems that morning at the religious commune, Wayne sitting like a dozing pit bull in the corner on a box, the tension in the room as Waylon won more and more (he soon had over ten thousand dollars in chips in front of him)—in a little while none of it was enough. Terry was too tired, too pulled out by the day, and he lowered his head on his chest and fell asleep, sound asleep, gone. . . .

20

He place-shifted in his sleep. It wasn't dreaming, exactly—more a belief that he was in some other place, at another time.

He was with his parents. They were on a trip (something they had never done) and they weren't fighting (also something they rarely had done, to *not* fight), and they had stopped at a small motel where his father went inside a room and came out with bundles of money wadded up in his hands, a big smile on his face. . . .

Terry awakened.

He was in the bed in the motel room. Sunlight was streaming in the windows. Between him and the door, Waylon and Wayne were sleeping on the floor, not in but on their bags, their breath coming evenly.

Terry propped up on one elbow and looked at the

two men. They were sleeping soundly, Wayne flat on his back, his mouth open, snoring softly. Waylon was half on his side, facing Terry.

Terry frowned. They looked so . . . so old. Waylon was nearly bald, starting to wrinkle, and Wayne had the beginnings of loose flesh under his chin that came with age, the way Terry's grandparents on his father's side had looked before they passed away. He had never met the grandparents on his mother's side. Two old men, sleeping on the floor of the motel room, two old—what was it Wayne had said?—dangerous men. Two old, very dangerous men. The thing that happened with Waylon, his eyes, when he became still and flat sounding—like a cobra. And Wayne sitting there on the box, coming awake like that, just because of the sound of a man's voice.

They had done things before. Together. Done very hard things, and a part of Terry wanted to know what it was they did and another part wanted to not ever know.

Wayne's eyes opened. He was looking straight at the ceiling and they focused at once, glanced first toward the door, then over to where Terry slept.

He smiled when he saw Terry awake and whispered, "You sleep good?"

Terry nodded and also whispered, "What time is it?"

Wayne looked at his watch. "Three."

"In the morning?"

"No. Afternoon. Waylon played until six. I carried you back to the room and you didn't blink an eye."

"Did he win?"

"He always wins."

"How much?"

"I don't know. Fifteen, maybe a little more."

"Thousand?"

Wayne nodded. "Yeah. It's a lot of money to take out of that little game. I thought we would have trouble, but Annie handled it all."

Waylon snorted and made a sound close to *gaack* and awakened. He sat up suddenly, looked around, then lay back down. "I could use some coffee. I feel like I've got a hangover."

"And food," Terry said. "I'm starving."

"First we have to do the money," Waylon said. He started digging in the pockets of his pants, which he'd slept in.

"Do what?"

"Bust it up." Waylon pulled wads of bills from both front pockets, then from both back pockets.

"How much did you win?" Terry asked.

"Just at eighteen thousand. I figure it comes to about six thousand each." He started arranging the money in three piles, stacking fifty- and hundred-dollar bills until they were about evenly matched. He handed one stack to Wayne, jammed one back in his pockets, and the other he leaned across and held up to Terry.

"You're giving me six thousand dollars?"

Waylon nodded. "Sure. You've got to disperse wealth or it doesn't work. What if we get separated?"

"But I didn't do anything. . . ."

"That doesn't matter. You were there, part of us, part of how we are."

"But six *thousand* . . ." Terry looked at the wad of money in his hand. "It's so much."

Waylon lay back. "It is—*only*—money. A way to store energy. That's all it is. You use it, live with it, don't worship the crap. It's just something to get you through the night."

"Let's go eat," Wayne interrupted. "We can always talk. My stomach feels like my throat was cut. It's OK to be hungry, but starving sucks."

They found a hamburger stand and ate burgers and fries and drank malts until they could barely move.

"So," Wayne said, looking at Terry, "what do we do next?"

"Me? You're asking me?"

"Sure. It's your turn."

"No." Waylon cut in. "It's nearly four o'clock—too late in the day for him to make the choice as to what we do next. He can start in the morning."

"Aren't we going to play more poker?" Terry asked. "I mean *you*. Aren't you going to play more? Wayne said you always win. Maybe you could win more and we would have even more money."

Waylon and Wayne looked at each other—again, that look. Like they knew something without having to talk about it.

"You never beat the game," Waylon said, and Wayne nodded slowly. "You go in, take what you need, get out. Never stay too long and never, never try to whip the game. Stay there too long and they figure you out, start chewing at the corners on you, know your betting. Then maybe two, three of them get together and whip-saw you."

"Whipsaw?"

"Bet against each other with you in the middle," Wayne said. "One might have a good hand, the other a bad one. The bad one raises the pot even though he knows he can't win, then the guy with the good hand raises and they keep doing that with you caught between them. Whipsaw. Later they split what they take off you."

Terry slurped the last of his malt. "Well, if we aren't going to play poker, what are we going to do?"

Waylon pointed across the street. "Wanda."

"What?"

"Wanda," he repeated. "See that doorway? It leads up a staircase to Wanda. . . ."

"Oh, man. Wanda isn't still here." Wayne leaned back and shook his head. "It's been twenty years."

"Some things, like love,"—Waylon smiled—"never die. I want the boy to meet her."

"Nobody does that anymore," Wayne said. "It's dangerous."

"Not to do—just to meet. He's too young for the other thing."

Terry listened to both of them, his head going back and forth like he was watching a tennis match. He was going to ask more but he was learning—slowly, he thought, but learning—and one of the things he'd learned was to not ask too many questions. They would show him what they meant.

Waylon looked at his watch. "Four-thirty. About time they got up anyway, don't you think?" He stood and went to the sidewalk, started across the street, and Wayne and Terry followed.

The door opened into a stairway and there was

another door at the top of the stairs. This second door was locked and Waylon knocked and stood back so he would show in the peephole at eye level in the door.

There was a moment's hesitation, a scuffling at the door, then a muffled woman's voice.

"He's too young."

"We're not here for that. We're looking for Wanda. We're old friends." Waylon pointed to Wayne and Terry. "These are friends of mine."

Another moment or two, then a clicking sound and the door swung open enough to let a large woman wearing a flimsy negligee fit into the opening. She was not fat, just huge—standing well over six feet—and to Terry she looked like a living mountain.

"I'm Betty," the woman said. "I knew Wanda."

"Knew?" Wayne had been leaning against the wall through the exchange and he stood straighter.

"Yes. She passed away three years ago."

"Ahh." Waylon sighed. "That's too bad. She was a good person."

"Yes. She was. Everybody who knew her loved her."

"She kept me from deserting," Waylon said. "I was stationed over at Rapid City for a while when I first went in the army—before I went to . . . school. I hated it and was going to split and she talked me out of it, talked me into staying in. I used to come here every week and she would sit and play classical music on that old Martin she had. . . ."

He let his voice slide off and for a long time they stood—the large woman in the see-through gown, Waylon, Wayne, and Terry—stood in silence at the top of the small stairway in front of the door and it was then that Terry realized what the place was, knew what Wanda had been.

"What got her?" Waylon asked.

"AIDS—what else?"

"Ahh . . ." Another sigh, deeper this time, sadder. "It gets so many."

Betty nodded, again there was silence, then she coughed softly. "Are you boys sure I can't offer you a little something?"

Waylon shook his head. "Not this time. We're just traveling through and I thought I'd say hello to an old friend."

"Well, then . . . it's cold standing here this way."

"We'll be going." Wayne turned to go down the stairway. "Thank you."

She closed the door and they were back on the street before Terry spoke.

"Were they—I mean was she, you know, a prostitute?"

Wayne said nothing, but Waylon smiled. "She was a lady named Betty. Other names don't count."

"Was Wanda one of them?"

"Too many questions," Waylon said. "The wrong kind. Wanda was a lady, Betty is a lady—why do you need other labels?"

"I guess I don't."

"That's right."

Waylon suddenly stopped dead and turned to Terry. "Ever hear of Wild Bill Hickock?"

Terry nodded. "Sort of. Wasn't he a marshal or something in the Old West?"

"Close. He was a drunk who could shoot a handgun

very well—and once was a marshal in Dodge City, Kansas. Mostly he was just a drunk. He died here."

"Where?"

Waylon poked his finger over his shoulder at a bar next to them. "Right there."

He led them into the bar and at the back there was a poker table, roped off, with cards lying on the top of it.

"He was playing poker," Waylon said. "Had his back to the door and somebody came in, walked up, and put a bullet in his brain."

"Aces and eights," Wayne said. "His hand. Two pair. Aces and eights. It's still called a dead man's hand."

They turned to go but Waylon hung back for a moment. "Clean . . ."

"What?" Terry asked.

Wayne went back to Waylon. Took him by the arm. "Come on, Wail . . ."

"So clean. In the head. It ended then, didn't it? Ended . . . right . . . *then.* Just clean and over. Head shots are so clean. . . ."

"Let's go, Wail," Wayne repeated. "Let's go now, come on." He made his voice soft, as it had been when they were at the religious commune. Like he was speaking to a dog. "Come on, Wail, let's go. . . ."

Waylon turned away from the poker table with the cards arranged the way they were supposed to have been the night Wild Bill Hickock was shot in the back of the head.

Outside they stood for a time, adjusting their eyes to the sudden bright light of the late afternoon sun.

"Looks like it's going to clear," Wayne said, still holding Waylon's arm. "Be a nice day tomorrow."

"Yeah." Terry nodded. "I'll have to think what to do."

"Why don't we go back to the room? Order pizza and pig out and watch television, then get an early start in the morning. Can you dig it?" Wayne led Waylon along the sidewalk, away from the bar.

"Sounds good." Terry followed.

"Maybe there'll be a good movie on. A western. I dig those old John Wayne westerns. The Duke—man, he could kick some serious . . ."

"He dodged." Waylon had stopped dead in the middle of the sidewalk and spoke suddenly, his voice soft but his eyes were back and his lips were in a half smile.

"What?" Wayne asked.

"The Duke. He dodged—skipped combat. Played all those hero roles and he dodged. Couldn't handle the freight, you know? Like the president. They talk good and wave the flag, but when it came time to pay dues they dodged."

Wayne shook his head. "Man, the Duke?"

Waylon nodded. "But I like the pizza part and getting an early start." He started walking ahead of them, as if the bit in the bar had never happened, his step light. "What are we going to do tomorrow?" he asked over his shoulder to Terry.

"I don't know. Anything. You know, about what to look for or anything."

"What do you want to know about?"

Terry frowned. "I'm not really sure. Maybe, you

know, what it was like, really like out here. Back before cars and highways and all of it. Maybe back when it was just Indians and cowboys. . . ."

"It never was," Waylon said. "Indians and cowboys. It was Indians and soldiers. This whole place, from here to Portland, the West—it was like Vietnam. A war."

"Then that," Terry said. "I want to start early and see something that would show me what that was like. What is there to see?"

Wayne said nothing and for a time Waylon didn't, either. Terry thought he was going to remain silent all the way to the motel room. But just as they stepped off the curb to cross the street to the motel Waylon stopped.

"Custer."

"What?" Terry bumped into his back.

"The height of it, what happened out here—it has to be Custer. The Custer battle."

"Are we close to that?"

"Half a day of driving, if the weather is good."

"Then that's it," Terry said. "We'll go there tomorrow."

21

THEY STOOD ON A HILL next to a group of small white stones and a large monument, a beautiful rolling prairie spread out before them, low and covered with knee-high grass leading down to a river lined with trees. It was all thick and green and soft. Meadowlarks sang around them and it was midafternoon and Terry tried to think of what it must have been like.

"The stones are where the bodies were found," Waylon said. "All white. They all looked white to the soldiers who came and found them. White against the green grass. Several men said that. They stopped a mile away and asked each other what all the white pieces were—they thought they were bits of paper. Scrap. Garbage. But it was the bodies. . . ."

The Custer battlefield.

They had gotten up early, well before daylight, after watching bad movies and eating pizza and going to bed before ten—this time Terry and Wayne slept on the floor and Waylon won the toss for the bed.

There had been no rain and they had driven across the Wyoming prairie with the sun warming their backs. There had been almost nothing to see until they pulled into Sheridan and had a hamburger, then fifty more miles up the highway, the Cat wheeling along in back of the Harley until they entered Montana and came to a sign that pointed up to the small hill.

"It seems like such a—I don't know, small place." Terry looked down the hill to the river. There were white markers scattered down a shallow ravine and he thought, *They died along the way, died trying to get up to this hill.*

"It *is* small." Waylon nodded. "Everything moved on horses then, slowly, and there was no artillery. Just guns and arrows. You had to be close to hit anything. All just a small engagement." He snorted. "Think of it. In the Gulf War with Iraq more people were killed in the first seven minutes than died in all of the Indian wars with all of the tribes and all the armies and civilians on both sides. . . ."

A tour came along, tourists following a guide. There was a building at the battlefield headquarters, where tour guides gave talks, and the three of them had stopped to hear one of the lectures and look in the museum. There were guns and pictures—there was even Custer's jock-strap in a case—but it didn't seem to mean anything to Terry until they walked up the little asphalt path with rattlesnake warning signs to the battle site itself.

The stones, Terry thought, *the white stones*. It was like seeing the bodies to him. *Two hundred and eighty some men just gone. In less than an hour, probably.*

"Snuffed," Wayne said, as if reading Terry's thoughts. He measured the ground with his eyes—to Terry it seemed like an engineer or scientist studying the ground—and nodded. "They must have thought they could hold if they got up here. Good terrain, high ground. Drop the horses and get down in back of them. . . ."

"Too many," Waylon interrupted. "Way too many Indians. Thousands. And smart. While the fight was going on, Crazy Horse took a big group of warriors back around the hill to cut off retreat and they swarmed up and over Custer and the rest of his men before they could set up a reaction. Bad fields of fire, bad perimeter . . ."

". . . bad luck," Wayne finished.

"That, too. All the bad luck there is."

"Poor bastards."

Waylon nodded. "Nobody won this one."

"What do you mean?" Terry turned from the stone marking the mass grave at the top of the hill. "I thought the Indians won. . . ."

Waylon shook his head. "Maybe this fight. But the battle set off a public reaction across the country—around the world. They lost any hope of a good settlement—if there ever was a hope. The United States came after them with whole armies, slaughtered them, drove them to the ground after the Custer battle."

"But wasn't it all the white man's fault?" Terry sat on a small corner of the monument.

Waylon nodded. "They broke treaties, took everything from the Indians—but it wasn't these soldiers who did that. It was prospectors, railroad tycoons, bankers—that's who stole the land. And these soldiers were sent to deal with it. Hell, most of them didn't even want to come out here. Irish immigrants trying to find the pot of gold in America, and the recruiters talked them into coming west. Custer's desertion rate was sometimes over ten percent per month. The soldiers were the losers. And the Indians, of course." He looked at the body markers, the prairie dropping around them. "Only the bankers won. And the politicians."

They spent the rest of the day at the battlefield, later moving down to the points defended by Reno and Benteen.

"They made it here," Wayne said. "Look at the shallow pits they dug when they established the perimeter. It was a bad defensive position but they made the best of it, and they held. Like it could have been another Custer but they held. . . ."

Terry smiled. Wayne seemed to be thinking like Waylon, in military terms and jargon. "You talk like it happened yesterday."

Wayne nodded. "Some things never change. They had different weapons. But they still had to have a perimeter, defensive positions, fire power, interlocking fields of fire. For the grunt it's always the same, no matter when."

Waylon nodded but didn't say anything, and instead led the way through this secondary battle site.

There was a small circular walk that led around to posts with written information on them, pointing to the different aspects of interest. Reno and Benteen had come in from different angles with their men, supposedly to support Custer, but they had run into overwhelming forces.

"One of the scouts said there were so many hostile Indians that the soldiers couldn't carry enough bullets to kill them all," Waylon said. "There might have been two, three, maybe even four thousand warriors—maybe ten or fifteen warriors to each soldier. Maybe more. And these guys held."

"How?" Terry looked down to the river. There were ravines, gullies for the Indians to use for cover. "Why didn't they run over these men like they did Custer and his men?"

Wayne laughed but there was no humor in it. A soft sound mixing with the meadowlark songs and soft buzz of flies. "Because they didn't want to. . . ."

Waylon nodded. "That's part of it. They worried that other soldiers were coming—bigger forces that would wipe them out. And they were right. So they fought here for the day, then gathered up their wounded and dead and left." He pointed to a range of snow-capped peaks in the distance. "Up there. They ran into the Bighorn Mountains and hid."

The peaks looked mysterious, beautiful. Terry had been watching them all day. "Can we go there next?"

"Into the Bighorns?" Waylon turned. "Into the mountains?"

"Yes. Could we go see them?"

"It's up to Wayne," Waylon said. "It's his pick next."

Wayne wasn't listening to them. He was looking

down the slope to the Little Bighorn, the river winding peacefully through the trees. "They say Reno like freaked, man."

Major Reno was the man commanding one of the groups that was supposed to support Custer.

"He did," Waylon said, nodding. "The man next to him took one in the side of the temple and his brains blew all over Reno's face. He couldn't handle it and started screaming, lost control completely, and his men took off, ran up this hill. . . ."

"Just from that? A hit on somebody else?" Wayne asked.

"Yeah." Waylon nodded. "That, and about a zillion Indians coming at him."

"Man, just a wound and he freaks."

"The kid wants to go into the mountains next," Waylon said. "You up for that?"

"What?" Wayne was still looking down at the river. "Oh, yeah. Sure. We'll head back down to Buffalo and cross there, get up in the high country."

"Cowboy country," Waylon said.

"Real cowboys?" Terry asked. Outside of a movie now and then he had never thought of them much. "Are there still real cowboys?"

"Right on," Wayne said, laughing. "Maybe we can find you a rodeo. Get *with* the guys with the big hats."

"And horses?"

"We'll try."

"Far out," Terry said.

Waylon and Wayne looked at each other and smiled.

22

THEY DROVE THE HIGHWAY back south down into Wyoming and at the small town of Buffalo they exited onto a smaller highway and stopped in town for the night at another motel.

"We can always camp," Waylon said. "Right now we're fat and it's going to rain."

Terry stood next to the car in the motel parking lot. It was late afternoon and there wasn't a cloud in the sky. "I don't see any rain."

"Old war wounds," Waylon said. "Aches and pains. The pressure is changing, which makes me ache, which means a front is coming in, which means it's going to rain. Besides, it always rains in the mountains."

"Ahh . . ." Terry nodded. "I should have known."

"Known what?" Wayne had parked Baby under an overhanging roof.

"About the rain coming."

"Not soon," Wayne said. "Four hours, at least."

"You, too?" Terry smiled. "You've got old war wounds?"

Wayne grimaced. "Hell, I *am* an old wound."

"I feel," Waylon said, throwing his pack into the motel room, "I feel the need for food."

"Café," Wayne said. "Down the street to the left. I saw it coming in."

Terry felt it as soon as they entered the café—a quickness to the air, a sudden tension. It was a narrow diner-type of building, a counter with stools and three booths. A man with a greasy T-shirt worked in back of the counter, cooking and waiting tables.

He nodded at the three of them when they came in but said nothing. Waylon slid into a booth and Terry moved in next to him, Wayne sat opposite them with his back to the rest of the diner.

There were four men in each of the other two booths, all cowboys, all relatively young, all in the same group, and apparently all drunk. Or near it. They had been talking, but as Terry and the two men came in the diner they stopped and watched the three of them sit down.

"Whoooeeee," one of them said. "They let anything into this diner." The speaker was wearing a large black cowboy hat—they were *all* wearing large black cowboy hats—and he stood to see better, talking to the man in back of the counter. "Don't you control it better than this? Letting this kind of thing in here?"

"Sit down, Carly—you're just bein' a no account."

"The hell I am. Look at 'em—that one is a biker. I don't eat with bikers. And the other one is probably a flatlander. God knows what the pup is. . . ."

Wayne was sitting still, both arms lying loosely on the table, holding a menu he'd taken from behind the napkin holder. He couldn't see the man talking but didn't seem to care what he was saying.

Waylon had looked up once but had gone back to reading his menu as well. To Terry both men seemed calm and unconcerned.

Terry was mad. They were insulting and rude and loud and stupid. "Why don't we go someplace else?" he asked. "We don't have to eat here."

"Don't sweat it," Wayne said. "They're just kids blowing. It don't mean nothing."

Waylon nodded. "All talk."

And for a moment it seemed Waylon was right. The cowboy's friends toned him down and things started to settle. The owner came from behind the counter with an order tablet. "I'm sorry about that."

Waylon shrugged. "Just kids . . ."

"They're bull riders. They were here for the rodeo yesterday. They've got two days to wait until the next one in Casper so they've been partying."

"It happens." Waylon held up his menu. "You ready to take orders?"

The owner nodded and they ordered hamburgers and fries and malts—were in fact nearly through ordering when the man who had been bad-mouthing them came up in back of the owner.

"You don't need to take their order," he said. "They were just leaving—weren't you boys?"

At this Wayne looked up. "I don't like that word."

"What word."

"*Boy.*"

"Well, hell, *boy*, you don't like it maybe you ought to do something about it." He pushed the owner sideways out of the way. "When you feel froggy, leap."

Wayne shook his head and smiled at Waylon. "I wonder who writes for these guys? 'When you feel froggy'?"

Terry couldn't believe how relaxed the two men were. The cowboy was tense, drunk, mean, but Waylon and Wayne were just sitting loose.

"Maybe *I* have to start the dance," the cowboy said. "Maybe I need to do a little jumping."

"It would be a mistake," Waylon said, looking up finally.

"I'm worried," the cowboy said. "Couple of old farts like you might tear me to pieces."

"I believe that was it," Waylon said.

Wayne nodded. "I was even going to let the *boy* go by 'cause he's drunk. But that *old fart* hurt me."

"So do something about it," the cowboy said, stepping back and raising his fists.

Wayne's left arm flicked. That's all Terry could see of it. A blur. The arm whipped away from the table and came back and Wayne was looking up to the owner. "Could we get onion rings?"

For a long second the cowboy stood, then his hands went to his groin and he grunted—deeply, a soul grunt—and he settled slowly to his knees. As his face came down, level with the table, Wayne's arm flicked again, and where the cowboy's nose had been there was suddenly a huge splash of red—*like a strawberry*, Terry thought, *had been crushed in the center of his face*. The cowboy's eyes crossed—he seemed to be trying to see where his nose had been—and he settled back on his rear end, then back against the counter, his eyes still crossed.

Waylon shook his head. "You could have killed him."

"I know. I'm out of practice—haven't been like this since the last time I saw you. You do bring out the worst in me."

The owner stepped over the cowboy—completely ignored him—and went to cook their orders.

"What did you do to him?" Terry asked.

Wayne shrugged. "Nothing much. Just a tap."

"His eyes are still crossed."

"Like I said—I hit him a little hard. I'm out of practice. He might be all right in an hour or so."

"Might?"

Wayne shrugged. "You never know. Some are tougher than others."

All this time the other cowboys had been relatively quiet, watching, but now two of them stood and came over.

"You didn't have to hit Carly that way—he was just funnin'."

"The hell he was. He was being insulting and teaching the kid here bad language. Like how to say *boy*."

"Still and all, you hurt him bad."

"Not as bad as he deserves."

"He'll come at you later, when he gets back on his

feet. Carly is one to come back at you that way. He don't like to quit."

Waylon cut in. "He comes back he'll get hurt worse."

"We might have to help him next time." There were some nods and Terry thought that they all looked tough. Wide shoulders, narrow hips, strong arms.

"Well, like the man said,"—Wayne nodded at the cowboy sitting on the floor—"when you feel froggy . . ."

For a second Terry thought the young man might do it, jump on Wayne. But he hesitated and then nodded at the others. "Come on, help me get Carly out of here." And they all picked Carly up and headed for the door where they stopped and the man who had last spoken turned.

"This ain't over."

"Yes," Waylon said, "it is. Please."

"Nope. We'll have to finish her. Carly will figure on it when he comes around."

And they left without speaking more. The cook came with their food, set it down without speaking, and they ate in silence.

Later they went to the motel, still without speaking, and they were unlocking the door when Wayne asked softly, "How many were there?"

Waylon stopped with his hand on the knob of the motel door. "Eight. Why?"

"Because there are three truckloads of cowboys sitting across the street. Must be eight or nine of them."

"They looking at us?"

"Yes."

"Ahhh . . ."

"They're going to wait and trash the car and Baby when we go to sleep."

"I expect so."

"Now wait a minute." Terry had been standing with his back to the street as well and he turned to see the cowboys. "This isn't fair. We'll have to call the cops."

"Think," Waylon said, "about what you said."

"Oh. Yeah." If they called the cops there would be questions. They would find out about Terry. "We can't call them."

"This is the wrong terrain," Wayne cut in. "They've got us cornered here."

"Agreed." Waylon nodded.

"I can't have them screwing Baby up."

"Nor the car," Waylon added.

"Right."

"So I guess we don't spend the night"—Waylon sighed—"in a dry room."

"Right."

"We run. . . ." Waylon offered.

"No." Wayne looked over his shoulder at the cow-boys one more time. "We seek a more defensible ter-rain."

Terry caught him out of the corner of his eye and was surprised to see he was smiling and that Waylon was smiling as well. There were eight men in the trucks, openly staring at them now, eight against two—*or two and a half*, Terry thought, *if we count me*—and these guys were *smiling?*

"Is the gas tank on the car full?" Waylon asked.

Terry nodded. "Close. Three quarters or better."

"Good." He opened the door and pretended to start in, then stopped and turned. "Here's how it will play. You go back to the car and get in like you forgot something, start the engine. Wayne will start Baby at the same time, and I will drop into the passenger side. We won't have a lot of time because they'll be on us."

"Where are we going to go?"

Wayne shrugged. "We need high ground. Just follow me and stay close. We'll head up into the mountains where we can find a position to defend."

"Why don't we run away?" Terry asked. "I mean wouldn't that be best?"

And again the look, the quiet look between them, and Terry realized with a shock that they didn't *want* to run away.

"But there are eight of them."

Wayne nodded and smiled at Waylon. "About right, wouldn't you say?"

Across the street the truck motors started and Waylon looked at Terry. "They're coming. I think it is time to execute the maneuver."

"But . . ."

"Now."

Terry turned and went to the Cat and thought all the way: *I get into this car and get her moving and I'm not stopping to fight, no matter what they say.*

He slid into the seat, turned the key, and the pipes jumped into life with a roar. At the same time he heard Baby fire off—the two vehicles deafening in the small confines of the motel parking lot—and in an instant Waylon was in the seat beside him.

"Drive." Waylon was looking out the side window.

"I think we ought to talk to them," Terry said, "or at least try to run. I mean, don't you really think it would be better?"

"Drive." Waylon pointed over Terry's shoulder and he turned in horror to see the front end of a three-quarter ton Dodge Cummins Diesel coming straight at him from the side. "Now."

Terry had the Cat in reverse and he pounded the accelerator and popped the clutch at the same time, slewed the Cat back and around just as the truck roared through where they had been parked.

He snapped the car into low, half floored it—worried that if he gave it all the gas the rear end would break loose—and the Cat snarled as they powered out of the parking lot and into the street.

"Right," Waylon said, his voice even. "Right and out of town . . ."

Terry nodded but didn't say anything. The rear end broke loose when he cut right—amazed that Wayne was already out ahead of him, the big Harley barfing so loudly he could hear it over the roar of the Cat—and he backed off a touch, shifted to third, then pounded his foot down.

The Cat leapt forward. The speedometer—he stole a quick look—seemed to jump from thirty to sixty and he caught fourth, watched it snap to seventy, then eighty, ninety, nudge a hundred, and would have climbed forever, fed by the turbo.

Oh, man, he thought—*Oh, man*—and he couldn't help smiling because in his mind he sounded just like Wayne. The Cat had come alive.

"A little more," Waylon said quietly. "Wayne is leaving us. . . ."

Terry couldn't believe the Harley. Wayne was pulling away from them, or was until Terry gave the Cat more gas. The car leapt again, 110, then 115.

"Good," Waylon said, looking back over his shoulder. "We're staying ahead of them."

Terry stole a quick glance in the rearview mirror and could see the pickups. They had turned out onto the street and were heading out of town but were clearly dropping back as the Cat picked up speed.

"A little more," Waylon said, again softly. "Wayne is pouring the coal to Baby."

The Harley was pulling away once more, but slowly, and Terry pushed another quarter inch on the accelerator, started nosing up on Wayne.

"One eighteen," Waylon said. "Hold it there."

Terry took his eyes off the road for a tenth of a second, saw the speedometer nearly pegged, then looked back to the highway. Out of town it went straight for a short time, then started climbing in gradual curves up into the Bighorns, and it seemed to be coming at them with an almost vicious speed. The dotted lines blurred into a streak.

"They'll never catch us now," Terry said. "Once we get into the curves we'll leave them like we hit warp speed."

"No," Waylon said. "We won't. The bike won't."

Terry took a curve to the right, powered out of it, centered the car. "What do you mean? We can't catch Baby the way it is now."

"A bike can't corner with a car. As soon as it starts

to get more curvy Wayne will have to slow down. . . . Ahh, see. There he is."

And he was right. Terry saw Wayne start into a curve, the bike leaning more and more until it could lean no more without dragging and he had to slow.

Terry backed off to match him and found the speed dropping below a hundred, then ninety, eighty. In the mirror he saw the trucks gaining. They were closer now, so that he could make out the figures sitting in the seats, lighted by the evening sun showing over the mountains.

"They're catching up." Terry pushed the gas but had to back off as they ran up on the Harley.

"Yes. We'll have to stop soon."

"Stop?"

Waylon nodded. "As soon as Wayne can find a place that he likes. I would think up on that rise to the right, where that small track turns off the highway—oh, good, he's seen it, too."

Wayne turned off the highway onto the small dirt path going up to a rolling rise of grass.

"Well, then," Waylon said, sighing. "There it is— as good a place as any."

"For what?" Terry asked.

"To stand. A person always needs a place to stand, and that's as good as any."

Terry shook his head but slowed and turned off, followed Wayne up the track until he saw the Harley stop at the top and Wayne drop the kickstand and get off carefully to move away from the bike and wait, his arms loose at his sides.

"Next to the bike. Slow there and then turn and leave."

"Leave—me? Why?"

"They aren't after you. They want us. You get out of this. Head west, keep trucking."

"I'm not going."

"Of course you are. Why would you stay?"

Terry stopped next to the Harley. "Because . . ."

Waylon smiled, jutted his chin at Wayne. "We're doing this because it is the way we are, have always been. It is our nature. Maybe because we want to do it. You don't have that problem. Now you leave."

Waylon slid out of the Cat, took his guitar and back-pack, and nodded at Terry. "Go. Now."

"No."

"Now. You'll be in the way."

"I will like hell. . . ."

"Just go. Before you get caught up here. . . ."

And it was, suddenly, too late. They had spoken too much, taken too long. In a cloud of noisy dust the three pickups arrived and the young cowboys boiled out of them.

Terry had one fleeting moment of what he thought later was insanity—the thought that maybe they could talk it out. He could get out of the still-running Cat and talk to them and stop what was going to happen.

But the men had not come to talk. Waylon put his guitar and pack down near Baby and moved to stand next to Wayne, slightly to his left and rear, and set one foot in back slightly. Wayne did the same thing, one foot back, and then the men were on them.

Terry tried to watch, tried to break things down in some order, but it looked more like slow motion dancing than fighting. Four of the eight men were slightly ahead and came in with fists clubbed, like they were trying to chop Wayne and Waylon down.

Wayne seemed to bend, push back on his rear leg, and when he came back up one of the men was down, holding his throat. Waylon swiveled at the hips, turned on his rear leg, and his arm floated out and another of the young men went down, his face a mass of blood and his hands hanging at his sides.

The other two hit Wayne and Waylon. Terry saw Waylon take the blow high on the right side of his head and rock with it, then come up with both hands in front, somehow swinging back and forth slowly and there was a meat-chunk sound and the man went down on top of the first.

Wayne was hit hard, low, in the groin, and even over the sound of the Cat's engine Terry heard him grunt. He started down on one knee but as his leg bent his arm came up and the man who had hit him seemed to lift a foot in the air, hang there, and then drop unconscious.

All this in seconds, two, not more. Terry raised in the seat and had opened the door—he thought to help, to stop it—and there were four men on the ground and Wayne and Waylon were still standing.

But they had been hurt and the blows slowed them and the next four, all in a pack, were on them almost at once, hitting and kicking them down.

Terry was out of the Cat now, gathered himself, and in one long jump piled in. He hit one man, used his knee to half kick, half push another off Wayne and then something hit him in the stomach—either a fist or a boot, he couldn't tell in the pile—so hard his whole life seemed to stop dead.

"*Uummmpppb!*" He turned, holding his stomach, sucking for air in a world suddenly gone airless, but his action had given Wayne time to chop up twice with his hands clubbed and another man was down, and then Waylon used a backhand blow to take down the sixth, and the seventh and eighth men were suddenly standing alone, facing the now-erect—though weaving—Waylon and Wayne.

Terry caught some air, held it, then a little more. Time stopped, held the four men. Wayne looked at Waylon, who was standing holding his left arm in place with his right, and he smiled.

Terry shook his head. Smiled. Crazy.

"Not bad for a couple of old farts," Waylon said. "Only two to go. . . ."

"Not us," one of the cowboys said. "We're whupped. I think you might of killed Carly this time— God knows he had it coming."

Waylon looked down and shrugged. "He isn't dead. . . ."

He was going to say more but a new sound came, keening, flat, and faint in the dusk.

Sirens. Somebody driving by had called them. Probably on a CB radio. The state police.

"Now you go," Waylon said.

"You come with me."

"No. They'll need someone here to talk to, tell our side. If we run they'll come after us and then you'll be part of it. You cut out now or they'll have you and that will be it. Go now. . . ."

And Terry could see he was right. If he stayed it

would help nothing. *Then this is it*, he thought—*this is all of it*.

He jumped in the Cat without using the door, looked once more at Waylon and Wayne standing in the pile of moaning and groaning cowboys, and snapped the clutch, throwing sand and dirt in a circle as he wheeled around and back out to the highway to hang a right and catch second, then third and fourth, and away, letting the Cat take him up the road into the Bighorns.

A mile. Then another and another, not looking back, remembering them standing on the hill next to Baby and the downed men and the trucks, and another mile, and three more.

West alone, he thought. *I'll find the uncle, see how that goes. I'll head west alone. I've got plenty of money and time, just head on out and see the country.*

And for a time he actually believed it. Five more miles passed and he kept making his mind believe what he was thinking. But it didn't work.

As if on her own the Cat slowed. Not to a stop but came off seventy, then down to sixty and fifty and forty and thirty, cars passing him while he kept saying to himself, *I'll head west alone, see the world alone. No problem.*

And the Cat stopped. In the middle of the lane it came to a dead stop, looking up at the Bighorn Mountains, summer snow catching the last of the evening light, and he knew then that he was lying to himself.

He checked the mirror, pushed the shift into reverse, swung around, and aimed the nose back down the mountain. Let the speedometer come back up to fifty, sixty, sliding along in the evening air.

The police would take them all back to town. That's how it would play. He'd move into town and watch, sleep in the car, until the police were done, and then pick them up again. It wouldn't be difficult to stay low and find them in the small town.

Alone, he thought, snorting. *Right.* Who would teach him to truck if he went alone? Besides, they owed him a choice day since they boogered his up with the fight.

He snapped the Cat into fourth and let her growl before he brought her back down to the speed limit, heading back into Buffalo.

If he worked it right this wouldn't set them back more than a few hours. . . .